I0822566

STRAWBERRIES and Diamonds

An Ellis Island Mystery

By Stephen Sparacio, Sr.

Order this book online at www.trafford.com/07-3053
or email orders@trafford.com

Most Trafford titles are also available at major online book retailers.

Cover and book design by Anthony Alexander

Note for Librarians: A cataloguing record for this book is available from Library and Archives Canada at www.collectionscanada.ca/amicus/index-e.html

ISBN: 978-1-4269-0023-5

We at Trafford believe that it is the responsibility of us all, as both individuals and corporations, to make choices that are environmentally and socially sound. You, in turn, are supporting this responsible conduct each time you purchase a Trafford book, or make use of our publishing services. To find out how you are helping, please visit www.trafford.com/responsiblepublishing.html

Our mission is to efficiently provide the world's finest, most comprehensive book publishing service, enabling every author to experience success. To find out how to publish your book, your way, and have it available worldwide, visit us online at www.trafford.com/10510

www.trafford.com

North America & international
toll-free: 1 888 232 4444 (USA & Canada)
phone: 250 383 6864 • fax: 250 383 6804
email: info@trafford.com

The United Kingdom & Europe
phone: +44 (0)1865 487 395 • local rate: 0845 230 9601
facsimile: +44 (0)1865 481 507 • email: info.uk@trafford.com

10 9 8 7 6 5 4 3 2 1

Dedication

To my wife Lucille for her love and faith in me, without which this novel would not have been possible.

For my daughter, Suzanne Soetje, for her expert typing of the original manuscript and cheerful words of encouragement.

For my son, Stephen Paul Sparacio, for his excellent efforts to do whatever he could to help me.

For my son-in-law, Frederick Soetje, for assisting with locating relevant information and checking corrections.

And for the millions of immigrants from many countries, including my father George and my mother Rose from Sicily who, in 1913, were brave enough to leave the known for the unknown land of dreams…

And, as I always fantasized in the past about writing these words, in the days when dreams were not yet real - "for Someday."

♦♦♦

Digital ID: cph 3a04881 Reproduction Number: LC-USZ62-1005
Library of Congress Prints and Photographs Division Washington, D.C. 20540 USA

Contents

Preface

"Give me your tired, your poor,
Your huddled masses yearning to breathe free,
The wretched refuse of your teeming shore,
Send these, the homeless, tempest-tost to me,
I left my lamp beside the golden door!"

Emma Lazarus, 1883

(From a bronze plaque on the Statue of Liberty pedestal - plaque now located in the Statue of Liberty exhibit.)

♦♦♦

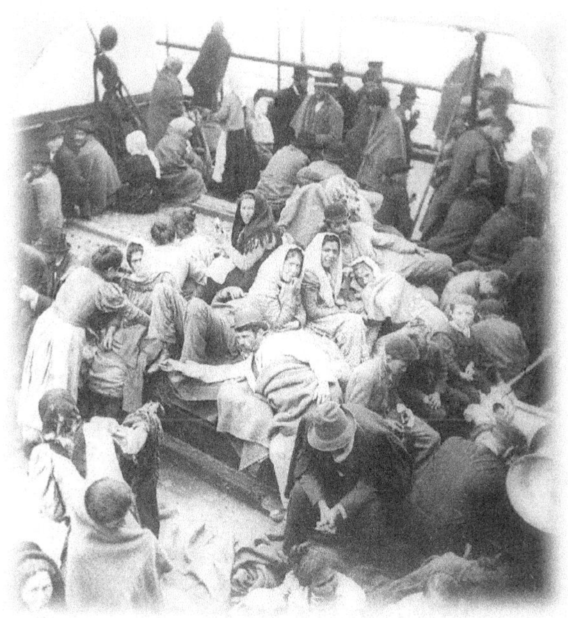

Digital ID: cph 3a09957 Reproduction Number: LC-USZ62-7307
Library of Congress Prints and Photographs Division Washington, D.C. 20540 USA

Prologue

The following story may be true - or it could be false.

If it's true, there is nothing further I can say because it would affect some of my ancestors and their descendants, obviously including me. If it's false, then there is no problem; fiction is fiction.

However, if you knew me or some of my relatives, you might - I said might - know more about the mystery and what really happened more than anyone else.

But, first you would have to go back to the year 1913 when it all began…

S.S.

♦♦♦

DIGITAL ID: cph 3g05584
Library of Congress Prints and Photographs Division Washington, D.C. 20540 USA

Chapter 1
Chen's Assignment

Chen moved quietly through the room on the red oriental carpet thick enough to muffle the heaviest of footfalls. Even though there was no need for caution, the assassin couldn't break the unobtrusive ten-year habit of stalking and eliminating his victims.

In the anteroom, there were four of Big Tan's bodyguards or "brainless thugs" as Chen described them. He had the same low opinion of Big Tan himself – the head of the criminal empire of drug dealing, prostitution, and extortion. If it weren't for his father, building and expanding this illegal empire which Big Tan inherited, Chen thought that Tan would have been just a short, thin, powerless, ugly man lucky enough to even be a taxi driver in Shanghai.

For an important reason, besides money, Chen endured Big Tan's arrogance and insulting manner. Masking his true feelings with the outward appearance of extreme loyalty to his employer, Chen knew that he was getting close to…

"Sit down, Peter," said Tan, pointing to a smallish chair in front of his outer office desk. The six-foot, 180 pound Assassin #1 (which Tan called him) squeezed into the chair and believed that he saw a sadistic smile cross Tan's face at his discomfort. Tan spoke softly and in an atypical conspiratorial tone. "This could be a big payday for you - and me - if what we learned was true."

"What's true?"

"It's a long story, but there may be a fortune in jewels, maybe, hidden on Ellis Island. Our information is that they were stolen and hidden in 1913. Believe that? If they were worth 3 million then, they're probably worth 6 million now, at least. I make much more than that in a year, but I can't ignore getting a few million more without too much effort."

"Without any effort at all on your part," thought Chen.

Tan believed that if Chen knew the real value today of the gems, he would disappear and keep them all for himself. An article, in the August 18, 1913, issue of the *N.Y. Times* archives, revealed that Rome police estimated their value at more than 12 million dollars. The researcher hired by Tan was later found by the roadside, apparently killed in a hit –and- run accident.

"Besides there's a mystery about where they may be hidden, and it's your job, if you're interested, to find out where they are on Ellis Island - if they really exist!"

"This could be a wild goose chase, Big Tan."

"Or it could be a challenging and very profitable mystery."

"What does this involve - flat rate or commission?"

"Because it does sound like a tough proposition, Chen, I'll give you 20 percent of what they're worth."

"Make it one third-33 1/3 percent."

"You know me well, Peter. Ok, 33 1/3 percent. You could make one or probably two million. That's if you find the jewels."

Chen couldn't understand why Tan was so generous. Possibly, he needed him again to do his dirty work or fool's errand and would have him killed even if he did find the jewels. Chen knew that the treacherous Tan would do anything for money. Chen smiled.

As Chen correctly assumed, Tan figured he could tell his Number 1 Assassin any amount, since, if he did find the jewels, Chen would be expendable. "Q" would take care of that.

"By the way, Big Tan, how did you find out about all this?"

"You'll find out in time, Peter, but I'll tell you a few things you should know, now."

Big Tan mistakenly interpreted Chen's thoughtful and intense look as interest and greed. But Chen was again remembering the past and the sacred vow he had made ten years ago in Shanghai…

Chapter 2
Beach Attraction

Steve Stanlee was restless not because of the hot sun or the uneven Jones Beach sand under his blanket, and certainly not because of the soothing and rhythmic ebb and flow of the Atlantic Ocean waves - but because he hadn't a case for the last three months.

After tracking down a n'eer-do-well who convinced the seventeen-year-old daughter of a Mafia Boss to run away with him to New Mexico, he spent most of his afternoons basking under the sun at Long Island's Jones Beach. His father, a recently retired New York City Police Lieutenant, had chided him for working for an underworld mobster. But his son had no qualms - a job was a job.

His father, David, used to regale him with stories about the syndicate, both Italian and Irish, and also the Chinese Tongs. In his 30 years as a police officer in Midtown Manhattan, he never ran out of stories. His mother Marian disliked her teenage son hearing about these crime stories even though her husband tried to exclude some of the more sensational aspects. However, sometimes in his enthusiasm, he neglected to omit lurid accounts about murderers, prostitutes, and other deviants. But, these stories never damaged his son's high moral code and strict Catholic upbringing.

Even though he was relatively new to being a private detective, by luck, word-of-mouth, and the recommendations of his father, he was involved in some notorious cases. A few were publicized in the three major city newspapers: the *N.Y. Post,* the *N.Y Daily News,* and the *New York Times* - and *Newsday* on Long Island.

When he was fifteen, he told his father that he wanted "to marry someone like Mom."

"I hope you do, Steve. She's the best."

Two years after graduating from Columbia University, his father noted that the playboy life style of his son wasn't leading to marriage. "Are you serious about any one of your parade of girlfriends? You know you're getting older and older."

"Maybe I'm too hard to please and can't find the right one."

"Maybe you enjoy being a playboy and all that stuff, Steve."

"I'm just not as fortunate as you were, Dad. I just can't seem to connect with anyone."

"Don't worry, when the time comes, you'll know."

"Will there be violins and the smell of roses and daffodils?"

"Don't be a smart ass. It'll probably happen when you least expect it."

"Is that what happened to you, Dad?"

"Yes, as a matter of fact. I literally bumped into your mother at a fraternity junior dance at Columbia College."

"Love at first sight, huh."

"Just about. Your mother has a different version of what happened. She said it took six months!"

Five years later, Stanlee was still waiting to hear the violins and smell the roses. His reminiscences were abruptly shattered by a sweet, gentle female voice above him. Could it be an angel, he thought whimsically.

"Are you Steve Stanlee, the private detective?"

Still sleepy and sluggish, he said, "Maybe… yes I am."

Stanlee looked up and saw, to his unexpected surprise, a beautiful, reddish-blonde-haired young woman - probably 21 or 22. As his eyes boldly moved down her body, he processed her firm breasts, long legs, and an extremely well-shaped body covered by a bright, one-piece blue bathing suit. Certainly a welcome intrusion!

"I'm Steve Stanlee, "he said. "What can I do for you?" He thought of a few things, but he quickly dismissed them as too inappropriate and too vulgar.

Before he was finished speaking, she was already kneeling on the blanket. "Can I sit down? The sand is rather hot."

"Of course. You look thirsty. Want something to drink?"

"I'd love it." The words sent a tingle-or whatever one would call a sexual thrill- through his body. "Coke, beer, or fresh lemonade. My mother made it. The lemonade, that is."

"Lemonade please." She looked at the ocean a few yards away and felt like jumping into it.

After almost a minute of intense appreciation of her body (which she was quite aware of), he asked, "What can I do for you?"

"I'd like to hire you. I'd like to tell you up front that it's kind of a strange case and story, maybe unbelievable."

"Well, I'll find out if it is. Start in the beginning, whatever that is."

"My name is Donna Martini. My friend and neighbor, Diane Foster, recommended you to me. She said she was in some of your college classes at Columbia."

"Diane Foster...Diane Foster. Yes, I remember her. She was in a couple of my English classes...or was it history?"

Stanlee remembered the energetic and aggressive short brunette who seemed always to be where he was. What a coincidence that the plump, sex hungry Diane might contribute to his getting another case, he thought.

"How'd she know I was here?"

"She said that in the summer you loved to come here by the ocean opposite Parking Field One. Diane said you liked coming here to relax and think."

"That's right." Stanlee would have added the many sexual trysts he and Diane had on this very beach one summer.

"She described you perfectly. She should've been a writer."

He wanted to hear how Diane described him, excluding of course, their sexual encounters, but he was more interested in Donna's body and her "strange, unbelievable" story. Donna was preoccupied with mentally verifying Diane's description: good looking, blue eyes, dirty blonde, tall, muscular, honest, thoughtful, very sexy, and a bit vain.

"What's so strange about your story, Donna? You don't mind if I call you Donna?"

"No. I'd prefer it."

After drinking a second cup of lemonade, she began. "I think I'd better start when it happened, in 1913."

"Long time ago."

"True. In 1913, my great-great-great uncle, Gaetano, sorry to say, robbed an upscale jewelry store in Rome, Italy, and tried to smuggle millions of dollars worth of jewels, mostly diamonds, into the United States. Actually about 12 million."

"A lot of diamonds. A lot of money!"

"Yes. To continue, on the immigrant ship, his friend, Guido, also from Prizzi, was killed by a Vallone's jewelry store detective who later probably murdered my great-great-grand uncle, Gaetano, on Ellis Island. In a letter to his brother Vincenzo, Gaetano said that he would hide the jewels on Ellis Island if for some reason he couldn't get them through Customs. He or Vincenzo or both of them would then come back for them."

"How did you get the letter, Donna? Why didn't his brother look for the jewels?"

"His brother died of a heart attack shortly after he received Gaetano's letter, and the letter was put into a trunk and miraculously was handed down from generation to generation."

"Sounds remarkable for that to happen. How did you get it?"

"My father happened to look through the stuff in the trunk, read it, and showed it to me. It was an exciting possibility and certainly a mystery. I wanted to check it out despite my father thinking it was probably a waste of time. Are jewels really hidden somewhere on Ellis Island? If so, their value today would be considerable."

"I would guess," said Stanlee, about twice as much, 24 million, if they were found, and if you kept them."

"That's another problem. I haven't figured that out yet. Who would own them - the Vallone Brothers jewelry firm or the State or the finder? Probably the company."

"One step at a time. What do you want me to do?"

"Read the letter and see if you could figure out where they are and then find them. I can't pay you much…"

"Don't worry about it," he said, and once again looked her over and thought lasciviously of a non-monetary payment.

"But, if you do find the jewels, if they exist, you could probably get your fee from selling the jewels or a reward from the original owners."

"We'll see, Donna." Stanlee opened up a bottle of Heineken beer for himself and then offered her another lemonade.

"No thanks. I've had enough."

Donna again noticed Stanlee admiring her and, apparently from what she thought she knew of men, was visualizing her nude. She imagined that other men probably did it, but this time, for some reason, she liked it and didn't mind.

"The two thieves, you say, were from the same town?" asked Stanlee.

"Yes. From Prizzi, in western Sicily."

"Prizzi… what kind of name is that? Does it mean anything, Donna?"

"My father told me it's derived from a Greek word meaning 'fire'."

"Sounds a bit ominous. I hope it's not a bad omen!"

"Now, one last thing, Donna. You say Gaetano is your great-great-great uncle?"

"Yes. I'm not good at figuring out relationships of ancestors, but I think so. He's the brother of my great-great Grandfather, Vincenzo. I had a problem even today about who's a 3rd or 4th cousin!"

"There are a lot of 'greats' in there. What do I call him? 'Great-great-great uncle?' Or 'brother of your great-great-grandfather?' Or 'Ancestral uncle' or just plain 'Gaetano' "?

"Not that it really makes a difference, but now that you've mentioned it, I like the last two. They're short and simple to say."

"OK, Donna. I'll call him by his first name or ancestral uncle."

"Now that's decided, tell me more, Donna, about this mystery which you say began in 1913." It would be a mystery which would end with the biggest challenge of his life- and perhaps his last.

Chapter 3
Steerage-1913

In the cheaper steerage section in the bowels of the ship, SS Stampalia, living conditions were intolerable. Because of his aggressiveness, Gaetano Martini had claimed a special berth fortuitously separated from the others and partly hidden in an alcove. The other immigrants had to contend with sleeping in two-tiered berths and would sometimes glance jealously at Gaetano's single and semi-private pallet-which originally was probably used by a high ranking sailor assigned to supervise the hold.

Each bed had a straw-filled mattress covered with a thin, white blanket and surprisingly and unexplainably without pillows. The two-tiered berths were close to each other with the only semblance of privacy being three-foot high wood dividers.

In addition to the extremely cramped sleeping conditions in the cargo hold, Gaetano couldn't understand the logic of covering the floor with fine sand one day and removing it the following day. The dusting of sand certainly didn't help the breathing of the immigrants and could also contribute to other health problems - and thus the sand, he concluded, seemed to serve no positive practical purpose.

The constant and unremitting smell of sweat and vomit and other odors, never mitigated with disinfectant, were sometimes so offensive that Gaetano and the other immigrants sought relief outside on the deck, weather permitting.

The ship owners apparently cared only about profit and not the personal welfare of each immigrant. The profit resulting from money invested and expenses in one year was their primary and only concern. The net profit was based partly on charging $35 per immigrant in steerage. It was the cheapest cost sufficient to provide the least expensive food and practically non-existent attention to the living quarters. Of course, the sizable profit made by the ship owners was also derived from charging much higher prices, sometimes as high as $100, for the private and more deluxe rentals of cabins above the decks of the steamship.

In was estimated that ship owners made more than $50,000 per trip, a large sum for 1913. The owners monitored costs so strictly that they calculated that they could feed an immigrant for as little as 60 cents a day. From 1890 to 1930, at the expense of immigrants enduring such inferior accommodations, entrepreneurs became wealthy by transporting sixteen million immigrants across the ocean, mainly from Europe and Asia, usually, but not exclusively, to a landing point at the southern tip of New York City or to nearby New Jersey. Immigrants from Asia were transported to ports in California and the State of Washington.

Gaetano wondered what had happened to his friend, Guido, who just a few hours ago must have been separated from him when the directionless crowd, in order to claim particular convenient berths, surged into the former commercial cargo section of the ship. The unsupervised stampede must have been too much for the little fellow who probably ended up on the other side of the hold and furthest from the Washrooms and the exit stairways leading to the main deck. He would look for Guido later.

Gaetano's thoughts were interrupted by the urge to urinate, a prostate problem plaguing him since his late teens. He quickly walked to the closest of three nearby makeshift lavatories, or "Washrooms," as they were called on ship, and went into the one marked "Men." To his surprise and disbelief, there were men, women, and children there. Embarrassed, he retreated and went to the next Washroom where he encountered the same situation-both genders using one Washroom. Before it was too late, he rushed into a stall and relieved himself.

As he tried to inconspicuously leave, he noticed that, in addition to the stalls, there was a row of urinals next to some sinks and also large white basins for washing small articles of clothing. The basins, he later learned, were also used for people who became seasick or for washing extremely dirty clothes or for other unsanitary reasons. The thought had repulsed him.

As each day passed, the living conditions were unrelentingly worsening. No ventilation produced stagnant and almost unbreathable air. The hold was never cleaned or washed and, except for the every other day floor dusting, received no further attention. Adding to the stifling air was the ever present smell of sweat and body odor from some immigrants who never washed themselves or who never changed their clothing during the two-week voyage. Gaetano was fortunate to find a kindly old Sicilian woman who washed and neatly folded his used clothes for a reasonable charge once a week.

As far as he could remember, his mother insisted that he wash every day and always try to wear clean clothing. His poor family shared whatever little food they had, and he suspected that sometimes his parents went without food. As an adult, he came to understand the sacrifices his late parents made on behalf of their two sons, Vincenzo and Gaetano.

In the hold, what offended Gaetano the most was the disgusting mess, usually urine or feces that children, and even adults, made when they couldn't reach the Washroom in time. Some didn't return to clean up the area, either not caring or hoping that other immigrants would do it for them.

Needless to say, in such close quarters and terrible living conditions, each day brought its inevitable share of brawls and obscene name-calling. However, the majority of immigrants, as observed by Gaetano, tried to wash almost every day and be as clean as they could be under the circumstances.

When the situation in the hold became unbearable, Gaetano, like many other immigrants, unless it was raining hard, would retreat to the deck to revel in the fresh ocean air and the periodic cooling, soothing breeze of the wind. On the deck, Gaetano would observe the other immigrants and note that his clothing was similar to that of other men: dark trousers, white shirt, short jacket, and wide-brimmed hat. He disliked wearing a long overcoat or head cap. A few men, out of habit or necessity, on boarding the ship wore formal suits with regular or bow ties; after a day at sea, the ties and suit jackets were soon removed but saved in their suitcases.

The women in 1913 were conservatively dressed, and any bare skin showing below the neck was deemed unlady-like and indecent. Most of them wore simple long dresses, head kerchiefs, straw or puffy-like wide hats, and long unrevealing shawls. The children were similarly dressed like the adults except some of the boys rebelled at consistently wearing head caps.

Weather permitting, Gaetano on deck would spend hours either talking to Guido at their early afternoon meeting place or thinking and staring at the boundless ocean, always securely holding his large leather satchel.

Gaetano and Guido Nuccio were two of the nearly 4 million Sicilian and mainland Italians trying to come to America between 1890 and 1914. In 1913, more than 100,000 of them were admitted into the United States. But, he wouldn't have been among that aspiring but yet unadmitted group if it weren't for Guido's bold plan-and his companionship, persistence, and optimism. He knew that he certainly would never have dared to burglarize the jewelry store and have the determination to reach America if it weren't for his good friend.

The name Ellis Island seemed to be imbued with some kind of magic as well as the promise of a future he thought would always be just a dream. If it were not for Guido's daring vision and imagination, he certainly wouldn't be on this ship heading toward America.

But, sometimes his mind would drift back to remember not only his late parents but also the warm August weather in Sicily and the holiday-like late August group celebrations after the grapes and other crops were harvested.

Gaetano would even miss the annual Easter Sunday celebration called "I diavoli a Prizzi" (The Prizzi Devils Dance and Race) which had frightened him as a young child. In this street event, citizens posing as Angels and God triumph over the masked evil devils and death. It was a symbolic battle between good and evil. Sometimes he would try to block out these nostalgic memories because they always made him cry, but he never could.

Chapter 4
Problems

Holding tightly the large traveling bag and standing at the deck railing, Gaetano looked at the seemingly endless Atlantic Ocean. Since he boarded the immigrant ship, the S.S Stampalia, he had seen the relatively tranquil and sunlit Mediterranean Sea replaced by a more vast and turbulent Atlantic Ocean. If Gaetano, or Guy as Guido sometimes called him, understood metaphors he would say that he left a placid but poor existence to one more treacherous and unpredictable.

The Stampalia, built four years earlier, weighed almost ten thousand tons, measured 470 feet x 56 feet, and had two funnels, two masts, twin screw, and a speed of 16 knots. Compared to most other immigrant steamships-turned-cargo, it was relatively new. Historians record that, four years later, on August 17, 1916; a German submarine (UB 47) sunk the Stampalia in the Aegean Sea.

He waited patiently for Guido at their agreed upon early afternoon meeting place in the farthest starboard and stern section of the ship. Perhaps it was best that Guido had not arrived on time because two men were lingering nearby, and Gaetano didn't want them listening to their conversation. Finally, the tall man with a red cap and his shorter companion ambled past him toward the middle of the vessel. The man in the red cap brushed slightly against Gaetano and muttered "Mi Scusi. Buono Giorno," and a few more conciliatory words. Gaetano, a Sicilian, knew immediately that the taller man's dialect indicated that he was mainland Italian.

Gaetano returned to his private thoughts. The year 1913 should be a more promising and richer one if he and Guido were able to pass through Customs at Ellis Island with the more than twelve million dollars worth of jewels that they had stolen from the world-renowned Rome jewelry store.

The thought of stealing always bothered him but the prospect of unimaginable wealth comforted him. For twenty-eight years, he and his brother, who emigrated to America two years ago, and their parents were some of the poorest inhabitants of Prizzi, a little town in western Sicily in the Province of Palermo. There weren't many jobs available in this centuries-old once feudal town situated on the side and top of a high mountain, 1045 meters above sea level. It was miraculous that the town for hundreds of years had survived marauders from the neighboring countries, particularly France, Greece, Spain, and Turkey.

Gaetano had to fight off nostalgia and homesickness when he thought about Prizzi. He knew it was easier, however, for him to leave with Guido after his parents died last year and after his older brother, Vincenzo, had left earlier to live in New York.

He was always comforted when he thought about how rich he and Guido would be after they sold the jewels, mostly diamonds, in America. The prospect of wealth fortunately sustained him and usually blocked out any negative thinking. He had always considered himself a moral and honest man and rationalized that the desperation of poverty and the desire for a better life justified his serious criminal act. Anyway, in America, he would confess to a Catholic priest to cleanse his soul.

His reverie was interrupted by Guido's annoyed words. "It's about time those two guys went away. Usually nobody ever comes here, Guy."

"Probably because they dump the garbage every morning over there. A terrible smell." Gaetano gestured toward the stern's fantail, shaped like a duck-bill, where crew members unceremoniously dumped the previous day's garbage into the ocean. The smell usually lingered for a few hours. "It smells OK by the time we get here, Guido. Good thing nobody likes to come here."

"Yeah, we can talk without anybody hearing us. There aren't too many places we can go for privacy - not with almost 2000 people on the ship!"

"True, Guido. On the food line, this morning, you said there was something important you had to tell me. You sounded upset. What is it?"

"An old Italian man told me he had been to Ellis Island before, and there were three major problems we had to worry about. First, though, he told me about the buildings there and the general layout which I'll tell you about later."

"Fine, what problems?"

"If you're not healthy enough, they can send you back to Sicily."

"We're in pretty good shape, Guido. I don't think that'll be a problem. What else?"

"They ask you if you have some kind of skill or trade that'll help you get a job in America."

"No problem. Nothing to worry about. You were a barber and a maintenance worker. I was a carpenter or tried to be - and did some construction work."

"Right," Guido agreed. "But this is the big problem. The Customs people check your baggage, clothes, everything. They look for illegal stuff, like drugs. How can we explain all of those jewels? They'll tell the police in New York who'll tell the police in Sicily or Italy. God, Guy, they could send us to prison."

In Italy, Guido was able to bribe a Customs Agent who, for a price, would overlook certain baggage that was carried aboard ship. "We gave him a lot of lire to look the other way."

"I know, Guido."

"I don't know if we could do that on Ellis Island. Besides, it would be too risky."

They didn't know that a few inspectors at Ellis Island accepted money for not inspecting baggage and also extorted "special fees" or "special charges" from some easily duped immigrants, waiting in line to hopefully be admitted. Even if they had known that a few inspectors took bribes, they would still have been too afraid to take a chance.

"What are we going to do, Gaetano? It's a shame to come so far and…"

"Let me think about it. I'll think of something."

Guido had so much respect for and faith in Gaetano and his resourcefulness that he immediately felt much better.

Later, sitting on his bunk, Gaetano not only thought about what Guido had said but also about Guido himself. In many ways they were different. Gaetano was tall, muscular, and good-looking, and Guido was thin, small, and physically unattractive. His supposed childhood friends called Guido "ugly donkey." His ears, unusually big and laterally extended, had earned him that cruel nickname.

But, both friends were similar in that they were both personable and very intelligent. Ever since they met twenty years ago at one of the three outdoor water pumps in Prizzi, they became good and loyal friends. Both knew the sadness and hardship of having parents who sometimes cried at night when there wasn't enough food and adequate clothing for their children.

"I have to think of something-something," muttered Gaetano. Then in one of those illuminating moments people sometimes have, the idea came to him.

Chapter 5
A Daring Plan

With plenty of time to think in the hold, Gaetano reviewed what he and Guido had done in Rome. At first, Gaetano thought Guido's plan was unthinkable, immoral, illegal, and outrageous. He couldn't imagine his little friend capable of planning, let alone committing, such a daring, bold robbery-and in Rome of all places, where Gaetano had never been and would feel even more uncomfortable as a stranger.

A year before, in 1912, Guido, after much self encouragement, decided to explain his plan to Gaetano. In a little café on Via Baiatelli in Prizzi, the only one which had outside seating in the summer, Guido waited until Gaetano finished his black demitasse coffee. In the cool outside air of approaching dusk, he said, "I figured out a way to get rich and get out of this poor miserable life." Just then they heard bells announcing vespers at St. George the Martyr Church located several blocks away.

"Guido, you're on vacation from your job in Rome, and you're already talking like some Roman big shot."

"Do you hear the evening mass church bells, Guy? Consider it a good sign. But seriously, Guy, I've been thinking about this robbery for a long time-every detail. We can pull it off if we worked together."

"A robbery? Are you serious, Guido? I can't believe you! I'm shocked! Shocked!" Gaetano took a deep breath and then reacted to Guido's pleading facial expression. "But...For you, my good friend, at least I'll listen. But don't expect me to go along with any of your outlandish criminal daydreams. You're always cooking something up. Remember. I'm just going to listen!"

Guido sighed in relief and contentment that Guy at least was going to listen to his plan. "We can rob hundreds of jewels from a big jewelry store in Rome, where I work. They'll never know that they've been robbed until we're far out to sea."

"What sea?"

"The Atlantic Ocean. We've always dreamed about going to America. In fact, as you know, we've even saved some money-not much I know- to make the trip. We'll get on an immigrant ship probably in Naples and go to America with the stolen jewels - actually they'll be mostly diamonds - which the store is known for."

"You're crazy, Guido!"

"No, I'm not. It can be done. You know, the other people here, (waving his arms) think I'm some kind of an idiot. But, you don't. You know I think through things before I do something."

"I know, Guido - ever since I've known you, I realized that you were a very smart guy, very intelligent."

"Thanks. You're about the only one!"

Guido looked around cautiously and said, "Before I tell you the plan, I just want to remind you about some things in my life and why I want to do this thing. You know I don't want to be always insulted by people here or in Rome or anywhere. You know how the kids here bullied me even after I got out of the sixth grade."

The sixth grade in 1912 was the highest level of education in Prizzi. One needed a lot of money to continue his education at nearby advanced and elite schools. "As a kid," continued Guido, "I always appreciated your warning the other kids not to bully me and to leave me alone. They were afraid of you because you were so big. I never forgot it. How kind you were, Guy." Guido saw Gaetano nod in remembrance of helping him by chasing away the mean and cruel children who were teasing and insulting his good friend Guido.

"You know I tried to be a barber here in Prizzi, but after two years the boss said that the two barbers he had were enough, especially since another barber shop opened up on the other side of town and charged cheaper prices. He said, 'I can't afford you. Sorry, Guido.' I certainly didn't want to get another job and work in the salt mines in the Province Enna digging for rock salt and asphalt or sitting on a wagon with a donkey pulling a load from town to town. I'm not that strong or tough, Guy."

"Yes. I remember Guido. But don't be too hard on yourself. You were a pretty tough kid, too. And from what I know, not a bad barber."

"Yeah, and also good with the girls," he laughed. "No, not even with them. I wasn't like you, the handsome Gaetano. Although many times I wished I could be!" Guido remembered the bitter truth: girls in Prizzi weren't attracted to a short poor guy with an unattractive face framed by two exceedingly large ears.

"Anyway, as I said, the boss barber fired me. What the hell! I decided to go to Rome, like one of my cousins did. He said that, unlike Prizzi, there were a lot of jobs there. I went there and could only get a job as a maintenance man-cleaning up, polishing the showcases, emptying the wastebaskets, washing the floor, and a bunch of other lousy jobs. But, I learned all of the important things about the store, and I know we can steal hundreds - I really mean it… hundreds - of diamonds and other gems. And don't think I'm crazy. I thought about it a long time, and I know it can be done!"

Guido again looked cautiously around the outside of the coffee shop and said, "Let me tell you what I've worked out. We can do it. As I said, I've spent enough time on it." Gaetano, as a kindness to his friend, and despite his doubts and obvious strong reluctance, listened respectfully to Guido.

Guido in almost a whisper discussed all of the details about a daring and seemingly unbelievable robbery that Gaetano at first strongly objected to but later relented and committed himself to a robbery which would eventually become a highly publicized newspaper story not only in Italy but also in Sicily.

Chapter 6
Romance

Stanlee, in his blue and white-striped bathing suit and with sunglasses in his hand, waited patiently for Donna to arrive. Four days ago they had arranged to meet today at 3 pm at the plaza in front of the Jones Beach West Bathhouse Pool and the adjacent Snack Bar.

It was very unusual for him to literally count the hours and days before he could see and talk to a woman – but this time he could hardly wait to see her again. In talking about her to his parents, his father said, "Are you interested in her or in finding the jewels?" (He was tempted to add "or in her body.")

"You're kidding, Dad. I really like her."

"That's what you used to say about those other women that you dated- what's so special with this one?"

"She's not only beautiful - of course that counts - but she's smart, funny, and easy to talk to. I feel like I've known her for years."

"Oh, oh," said his father.

"What does that mean?"

"It means Steve that you may be falling in love…it's about time!"

"I only just met her. That's a bit of a stretch."

"I know you, son. I met your mother only once, and I think I know what you're feeling. I think you're a goner - about time. You're 28 years old… old enough to settle down."

"And how old were you when you got married to Mom?"

"Pretty soon after college. We were both 22. I didn't want to let her get away. Good thing or you wouldn't be here!"

Then he saw her striding down the walk toward the few steps leading to the plaza. He couldn't believe that he was so nervous and anxious to be with her again. As she came closer, he saw that the nearly blonde Donna was not wearing the one-piece blue bathing suit he had first seen her in, but a yellow bikini.

She also had felt the chemistry between them and today deliberately tried to be as sexy and as appealing as she could. So she had gone to Lord and Taylor in Garden City and was fortunate enough to find exactly the bikini she wanted.

Stanlee's eyes traveled unashamedly over her pretty face, slender figure, firm breasts, and very revealing and provocative bikini. His imagination went into overtime. She realized that he was impressed with what he saw, and that made her very happy. Her mother seriously had said, "If that bikini doesn't do it, nothing will!"

The reddish streaks in her blonde hair were gradually disappearing. The color red, except for the red color of strawberries, which he loved to eat, for some reason always bothered him. Someday, maybe, somebody could explain it to him.

"Hi, Mr. Stanlee. Sorry I'm late."

"Just five minutes late. And call me Steve. After all, we've known each other for at least four hours" (and what seemed a lifetime, he thought).

She laughed. "OK, Steve. I've been wanting to call you that, anyway. Could we go to the ocean and swim a bit. It's awfully hot."

"Sure. I'd like to cool off too." (he meant not only his body but his passion). Pointing to a wicker picnic basket, he asked, "What's that you have there?"

"Oh, I made some sandwiches, potato salad, and brought some bottles of Heineken beer which you seemed to like. I hope you don't mind."

"Are you kidding? I'm glad you brought them. I was getting hungry and thirsty. And as for me, my contribution is a bottle of Hearty Burgundy wine. I hope you like wine. I brought lemonade, also, just in case."

"Wine's fine," she said." I like wine ever since my grandfather taught my father how to make home-made wine. I still remember it. They would crush grapes, with my grandfather's large compressor and store the grape juice to ferment in wooden barrels lined up along a wall in our basement. My grandfather was always saying, "You can't beat home-made wine. It's stronger and tastes better."

At the water's edge, he placed the cooler with the thermos of lemonade and the bottle of wine on the large blanket. He put her picnic basket, which she had insisted on carrying herself, next to the cooler. He took out two ceramic cups and the chilled Hearty Burgundy wine from the cooler. Unlike some people, he liked his wine cold despite his wine connoisseur friends telling him that most red wines taste better when served between 58 and 63 degrees.

"After my Grandpa died, my father, without his father's help and enthusiasm, couldn't bring himself to make the wine anymore. He finished off the basement and was content to buy burgundy and sometimes Chianti in the liquor store. I knew he missed his father, especially when he would say, "It's not like what my father used to make." Stanlee related to what Donna said because it reminded him of the close relationship he previously had with his late paternal grandfather and how he would feel if his father or mother died.

"My father, like my grandpa, always had a glass of red wine with his Sunday dinner, and then demitasse coffee. Like a weekly ritual," said Donna.

"I sometimes do that, especially in the summer when I have beer or wine with a meal. But I never really liked liquor or even smoking cigarettes - my parents' influence."

"Same here," said Donna. She thought again that these little things made her feel that they seemed to have a lot in common. "Could we have the wine and sandwiches later, Steve? I'd like to cool off first. Seems like I always want to jump into the water when I'm at the beach! Then, if you want, we'll eat, and you can read my great, great-grand uncle's letter."

Before he could say "Fine, Let's go," she was already heading for the breakers. As he reached her, she began laughing and splashing water on his face. After recoiling from this unexpected but friendly assault, he retaliated but in a very gentlemanly fashion. They were both soon frolicking like high school kids. He later told his parents. "I felt like a teenager again. She's really something!" His mother and father had exchanged the usual parental knowing glances.

Finally, Stanlee yelled "truce" and then held her around the waist ostensibly to stop her from splashing him. In what he later described as an intuitive impulse, he kissed her and when she offered no resistance, he kept kissing her. Awed but pleased by what had just happened, they then walked, hand in hand, toward shore, knowing that all of a sudden their world had changed. On shore, they embraced and kissed again and again until they happily sat down on the blanket.

"Wow," she said. "I can't believe it all happened. I'm happy it did!"

"Me too. I guess I'm the luckiest guy in the world," he said even though he knew it was a cliché and didn't hear violins playing and flowers dropping from the sky.

After half-heartedly munching on sandwiches and sipping wine, they resumed kissing until she was getting too excited and said, "We'd better stop. We're not even engaged, not that it would make a difference. Remember, I'm a good Catholic girl."

"Consider yourself engaged, Donna, to a good Catholic boy."

"I accept, but we still better stop."

He knew he was romantically and sexually attracted to her, but he respected her wishes even though he noticed she was breathing heavily and that her breasts were straining against her bikini top.

"We'd better read the letter now," she said nervously and trying not to look at him and be tempted to ignite the passion again. "It's here in my handbag. The original's in here plus some copies I made."

"Is it in Italian or Sicilian? There's a difference, right?"

"There is a difference, Steve. Some words in Italian are different from Sicilian ones." For example, I think "Uva" is Italian for grapes, but it's "Racina" in Sicilian, and "bacia" is Italian for kiss and it's "vasa" in Sicilian. At least according to my father, Timothy. He's usually right, but I'll ask him again about it."

"Timothy. That's your father's name?"

"Yes, and there's no problem with the letter since he translated it from Sicilian to English."

"That I can handle, Donna!"

Stanlee was excited first with Donna and now for the second time that afternoon as he was on the verge of reading a letter written almost 100 years ago by one of Donna's ancestors and which might suggest the whereabouts of a fortune in jewels.

"Your great-great-grand uncle-or ancestral uncle- was murdered after he wrote the letter? Right?"

"Yes. According to another letter written by one of Gaetano's distant relatives in Prizzi, he was murdered in the main building on Ellis Island on August 14, 1913. They never found his killer. But, apparently it could be the same person who killed his friend, Guido."

"It's kind of chilling, Donna, to read a letter from the past and not know the man, your ancestor, who wrote it."

"Exactly how I felt. Here it is."

Stanlee after looking at it briefly, said, "The handwriting looks a bit shaky, Donna."

"I noticed that, too. I wonder why."

Stanlee then read aloud the two-page letter, dated August 10, 1913, slowly and analytically.

Dear Vincenzo,

It's very hard for me to write this letter my dear brother, but I must. Please read this letter carefully. Do you remember Guido, my childhood friend? One of the two Italian jewelry store detectives killed him and threw him overboard. The killer got mad because Guido wouldn't tell him anything.

When Guido, poor Guido, spit in his face, the Italian detective killed him. It just happened a little while ago. I still can't believe what happened. I'll tell you the whole story when I see you, in 4 or 5 days hopefully, after I get out of the Reception Center.

In case Guido's killer finds me or I can't get them through Customs, I'll have to hide the jewels on Ellis Island. Guido said they must be worth about twelve million dollars, American money. Do you believe that! If I do have to hide the jewels, I'll hide them carefully so that they won't be discovered and confiscated by the Customs inspectors or anyone else and then I or both of us will come back for them later.

I have to take a break now, Vincenzo. As you know, I have to go to the Washroom often. (Gaetano used the word "lavatoio" for washroom as it was called on the ship, instead of the more familiar phrase for bathroom which was "stanza da bagno.")

You know I have a prostate problem, Vincenzo, and that sometimes I have to urinate five times a night... Five times is too much! Five times!

In case I don't make it, I don't want anyone else to chisel, that's right, chisel you out of the diamonds and other gems. I want you to have them if something happens to me. So, again please read this letter carefully. I assume you probably got-or will get-my other letter which I mailed almost two weeks ago.

I hope to get through all this and see you in the waiting room after I get past Customs in the Reception Center-that's the main entrance building. Remember-the main entrance building. I've got to go to the men's room now.

Before I forget, congratulations to you and your new baby, Antonio. He must be about five months old now.

I love you, Vincenzo, my dear brother. I know you would wish me "Buona Fortuna."

Gaetano

Stanlee was so moved by what he had just read, in a letter written almost 100 years ago, that he tried to disguise his sympathetic feelings for this long deceased man who like him had grappled with moral sensibilities and who also was a dreamer. Somehow he felt a connection-an identification-with this man who died so long ago. He probably might have become emotional if Donna weren't there.

"Do you think he was able to hide them, Donna? Or did his killer get to him first?"

"We'll never know unless we try to find them. And that's your job, to solve the mystery, my sweet wonderful boyfriend."

"Engaged boyfriend."

"That's right, I said okay to that...engaged boyfriend." Then she kissed him with such fervor that if it weren't Donna, he would have been tempted to rip off the bikini and ravish her on the beach blanket.

At this exhilarating moment, it was fortunate that he couldn't visualize the future when a life-or-death confrontation between him and a deadly assassin would be decided when one of them made a fatal mistake.

Chapter 7
Grand Theft

They didn't know that they would soon become two of Italy's most famous but anonymous burglars. The Italian newspapers, and even some foreign ones, carried the story for weeks: "Daring robbers steal more than twelve million dollars of gemstones, mostly diamonds. Robbers still at large. Police are following up several leads. Vallone's offers reward." The headlines seemed never ending.

The two had met in Rome, and on the following Saturday night after they bolstered their nerves and resolve, they decided to steal the gems. "It's very scary, Guy. I always get afraid when I'm alone and on the midnight to 8 shift. I usually worked overnight only when the regular man got sick or went on vacation. There's also hardly nobody outside the building in this part of Via Vittorio Veneto, Rome's classiest avenue, and inside it looks even more like a ghost town," said Guido, trembling slightly.

"But I got used to the shift. I did my work, ate, took a nap, whatever. For some reason, they never had anybody clean or even guard the place on Saturday night - like tonight."

"Why not?" asked Gaetano also nervous and hoping he didn't get another panic attack.

"Who knows? Maybe they saved a day's pay or didn't expect any trouble or followed an old rule. Or maybe they just weren't too smart or efficient. Who knows?"

"Seems odd to me."

"But lucky for us, Guy."

As Guido had predicted, at two in the morning, there were hardly any people, citizens or tourists, outside the building. Guido motioned Gaetano to follow him to the narrow unlit alley between the large jewelry store and a smaller boutique which also catered to some of Rome's wealthiest women.

Surprisingly there was no alarm system in Vallone's in 1913. After the robbery, a simple but still ineffective system was installed - unlike the improved technological system introduced decades later.

"It's hard for me to believe they don't have any system here to protect against robbers."

"Maybe some day they will, but right now we're in luck, Guy." Guido used a long, thin key to open the outside side door. "The manager who thinks he is so smart and who's always insulting me leaves this side door key, the key to the special room and the showcase keys in his lower right hand drawer of the desk in his office. He even leaves the combination to the safe there. And he calls me stupid. I once heard him talking to the assistant manager about me."

"What did he say, Guido?"

"He said something like Guido's a pleasant enough guy, but I think he's stupid - a little slow - maybe retarded. He has a dirty job I wouldn't want, cleaning the bathrooms, emptying the garbage baskets and things like that. I guess it's the only thing he's capable of doing. But, as long as he does his job, we'll keep him."

"We'll see who's stupid and retarded now when his store is robbed of millions of dollars, and he has to explain it. There goes his job! And he won't know who did it!"

Guido pointed to the manager's glass-enclosed office in a corner in the rear of the store. "As I said, the manager, must be really, really stupid to keep all the keys and the combination to the safe in his desk, of all places! During lunch one day, when nobody was looking, I took the two keys, for the outside door and the special room, which I had duplicated by a locksmith down the street. I also copied the combination to the safe. I put back the keys and combination when I had a chance to, after lunch. Now, who's stupid? The big shot manager is very dumb - or lazy - to leave such important keys and combination to the safe in his desk where anyone - like me - could find them!"

"Doesn't sound like a very nice or smart guy to work for? Guido, we better get moving. This is making me too nervous. I feel like somebody's going to come in any minute and see us."

After unlocking the door to what was called the "special jewelry key room," Guido kneeled in front of the safe. He flicked the dial of the safe, referring to the numbers on a piece of paper. After flicking seven numbers, he opened the safe. "I didn't know you were a safe cracker, too." said Guy.

"No problem. It's easy. You could do it, too," said Guido laughing. I'll lock everything up later, "said Guido. "I guess since you like diamonds, we'll start with them. These are the keys to the fifteen showcases there. I'll take the other side."

"Yeah, diamonds sell for a lot anywhere in the world, Guido."

"Especially in America." said Guido." We should take just enough so that the salespeople won't know they're missing and won't be suspicious. By the time they find out after taking inventory next Friday, we should be on the ship to America." Very quickly and methodically they scooped hundreds of diamonds - large and small -expensive and very expensive-into large canvas bags.

"OK, Guido, I think we have enough. Must be hundreds and hundreds! Let's go."

"Wait. Wait. As long as we're here, let's get some of the other gems besides diamonds."

"Like what?"

"Over there are rubies, pearls, emeralds, jade, dark red garnets. Forget the watches. Wait, I'm going back to the jewelry room. I almost forgot! They also have a special place in the safe where they hide the very, very expensive diamonds. God, I can't believe I almost forgot! I'll be right back."

"OK, but hurry up, Guido. We're pressing our luck."

Guido came back, red-faced and breathing hard, put the showcase keys back in the safe, twirled the dial, and then before he said "Let's go," he told Gaetano some astounding news. "It's fantastic! Unbelievable! How stupid...really stupid...the store bosses are. I forgot, but then I remembered that in a compartment in the bottom of the safe are some of the world's most expensive diamonds-for their Fall sale. They buy them in June and July from estate sales and also from very wealthy people all over the world. They were in a large leather bag. I think its called morocco."

"What exactly was in there, Guido? Tell me. You got me all excited, too!"

"There were eighteen of the world's most expensive kinds of diamonds in four of those soft - what do you call them - soft drawstring felt pouches."

"God, Guido. What are you talking about? How expensive are they?"

"Each diamond-are you ready?-each diamond, from what I was told last year about the same type of diamonds, is worth about $500,000 dollars - half a million in American money. Each one! I can't believe it. It's like a miracle! Millions of dollars worth of diamonds in a little safe! And I almost forgot about them!"

"My God, Guido. We could live a lifetime with one of those diamonds. No, twenty lifetimes!"

"Here, Guy, look at them. Look at the colors. I know all about them. They talked about them a lot last Fall, and I remembered they had brochures with pictures of the different colored diamonds. In fact, they were there in the safe, and I took one of them. They won't miss one!"

Guy looked at the new brochure and was dazzled by the pictures of the diamonds and their colors: red, blue, green, and purple of varying combinations and intensities.

"They're called "intenso´ diamonds," said Guido, showing off his knowledge. "They're very strong looking, very deep. Rare diamonds."

"Who could afford to buy these diamonds?" asked Guy.

"You know who, Guy? Certainly not people like us except we have them now. Kings, queens, princes, princesses, other royalty, big-shot businessmen, other rich people. They can afford them. What a shame! All eight hundred or so people in Prizzi could live in luxury for years on what these diamonds would sell for!"

Guido looked intently at Gaetano. "Are you surprised that I know so much about these diamonds, and that we're going to pull this off beyond our wildest, wildest hopes!"

"I never doubted you, Guido!"

As they hurriedly went out the side door, Guy asked, "How much do you think all of this is worth, roughly?"

"I'd guess about twelve million dollars, maybe more. We'll be fantastically rich, Guy."

For the first time in his life, Gaetano felt a sense of security and confidence mixed with hope for the future. But, at the same time, his conscience started asking him some ethical questions.

"I always knew you were a smart, sharp fellow, Guido."

"I know you did, Guy. I know you did."

And they disappeared into the darkness.

CHAPTER 8
CHARLIE

Early in the morning, he picked up the phone after it rang several times. "Hi Donna, honey, what's happening?"

"As you know, I couldn't see you yesterday since my parents and I went to a cousin's engagement party."

"Yeah, you told me. Maybe we're next."

"Keep thinking that way. Maybe we should start planning it?" asked Donna, delighting in teasing and testing him.

"Great idea!" With that response, she definitely knew he was truly serious about her and marriage.

"First we have to take care of finding the jewels. Now I have some unusual news. When we came home last night, our house was ransacked."

"You're kidding. What happened?"

"The strange thing," Donna said, "is that they took nothing of value. What kind of thief would go through all that trouble without taking anything?"

"Are you sure the thief, or whoever it was, took nothing?"

"My parents and I checked everything we could before and after we called the police."

"You know, Donna, I think...Do you still have the letter? But how would somebody know about it, anyway?"

"The original and the copies are still in my handbag... This is kind of weird, but now that you mentioned the letter, I think my brother Charlie might be involved."

"What could he have to do with it?" asked Stanlee.

"Charlie enlisted in the Army about a month ago, and his friends gave him a farewell bachelor party in the city last week. After they hit a few bars, they thought they'd give him a treat so they brought him to a massage parlor called the Golden Palace, on 47th Street, which he said really didn't give massages."

"Got it."

Charlie admitted to me before he shipped out to France a couple of days ago that he was so drunk he told the girl...there....the...er."

"Probably a prostitute."

"Right. He told her he might be very rich if diamonds hidden a hundred years ago were found. The girl...prostitute...there...was named Yvonne, I think. She listened to him, he said, very carefully and, even though he was very drunk, he remembered she asked him a lot of questions, including where the letter was."

"Charlie was very embarrassed and ashamed and hoped that he didn't cause any trouble and pleaded with me not to tell our parents. My guess... and perhaps it seems farfetched... is that they were after that letter."

"Did your brother say how much he thought they were worth?"

"Yes. He said he could live a long time on twelve million dollars."

"Could be it, Donna. On another note, how about dinner tonight at the restaurant I told you about-Nick Diangelo's on Sunrise Highway in Merrick? It has great food, wonderful décor. In addition to the general public, a lot of celebrities from Long Island and New York City also go there. I know the owners, Ralph Moccio, and his partner, George Kortner. Really nice gentlemen. If Mr. Moccio's there, I'll introduce you to him. We'll talk then more about what happened."

"Fine, since you say the restaurant's so terrific, I might have one of my favorites-T-Bone steak, well done, or maybe linguini."

Stanlee had a difficult time ticking off the hours until he would see Donna at 7 pm. He shaved, showered, dressed, had some eggs, read the local newspaper, *Newsday,* left at his front door, watched TV'S morning "Fox and Friends" on cable channel 26 (he liked the combination of news, interviews, humor, and sports updates) until finally at 6:40 pm he headed for Merrick in his royal blue Jaguar. Thinking that she was late as usual, and that he would have to wait, he handed the keys to the always cheerful valet and then happily spotted her white Toyota Camry in the adjacent parking area.

"Finally on time, "he said to himself smiling. In the restaurant lobby waiting area, she said, "Hey, you're late, Steve."

"Just a couple of minutes, Donna. Let's go in. I'm hungry."

"And thirsty."

For dinner, instead of steak she ordered another one of her favorites - linguini with white clam sauce with whole shell Little Neck clams - and he asked for the most expensive cut of Filet Mignon, sliced, with garlic mashed potatoes, and stir-fry vegetables.

"I'm glad you're paying for it, "she said.

"No problem! How about something to drink, Donna. What would you like? House wine? Burgundy? Soda?"

"I'll have burgundy. Perhaps we should get a carafe," which the hovering nubile young female waitress duly noted.

Stanlee was in such a good mood that he drank more wine than he usually did.

"Hey, that's your third glass of wine. I hope you don't get any ideas about getting me drunk. I'm still a good Catholic woman, as you know."

"I know. Don't worry. I just feel good being here with you."

"Oh, that's OK. I feel the same way."

"If I have another drink, Donna, I might officially propose!"

"Keep drinking," she said.

"I'd like to wait a few months."

"Is this a delayed proposal?"

"I think so. Let's drink to it," he said.

"You know, Steve, I forgot to tell you this morning that Charlie thinks he heard...Yvonne mumbling something about telling "Big Tan," whoever that is, probably the Boss, about what he said. I can't ask Charlie since he's on an Army troopship bound for Germany where he'll then go to France."

"You know, Donna, perhaps this Big Tan - what an odd name – sent some men to find the letter in your house."

"Could be. I'm glad we weren't home. Who knows what could have happened?"

Stanlee said that tomorrow he would go to the Golden Palace and see what he could find out.

"Don't stay too long. I don't want you to get tempted."

"No way. Prostitutes aren't my cup of tea."

Chapter 9
Kidnapped

The next day in the late morning, he drove into Manhattan, left his Jaguar (with some trepidation about its safety from damage) at a nearby parking garage after paying the $33 fee.

After walking two short blocks on 47th Street, he stopped in front of a narrow building squeezed between two other buildings which were marked "For Sale." Above the door was a sign "Golden Palace" with each letter in a different color. Underneath it was a smaller sign that advertised "Personal Massage Service."

Stanlee entered a dimly-lit anteroom so small that he almost bumped into a desk behind which sat a plump, stern-looking receptionist. With a quick glance, she favorably sized up the tall, handsome man in front of her who didn't seem like the usual type of customer. But, after two years of working there, she was used to anything walking through the front door.

"Are you a cop, buddy?"

"No, do I look like a cop?"

"Yeah."

"Well, I'm not. I'd like to talk to…see…one of your…err, therapists, Yvonne."

"You're lucky, mister. She happens to be here today."

"Fine."

"That'll be 100 bucks for forty minutes."

"That's pretty expensive for a massage."

"Not the kind she gives. Yes or no? I don't have all day."

"OK." Stanlee took out his wallet and handed over two 50's.

"She's down the hall on your left. Number 8. I'll buzz her. And no funny stuff or you'll have to deal with Dolph there." For the first time, he noticed a rather large, awesome-looking brute sitting behind her desk in the corner shadows.

He pushed aside the bamboo curtain below the number 8 and saw the very comely brunette sitting at the edge of the bed, legs crossed, and wearing a loose, wide-sleeved light green robe with an even darker green sash.

"Are you Yvonne?"

"Yes. Didn't Mildred tell you?"

"I was just making sure."

"And you're?"

"Steve."

"Well, Steve, what would you like? Anything goes."

"If it's all right with you, I came here for some information. That's all."

"Too bad, fella. It would have been fun. I hope I can tell you what you want to know-whatever it is."

Stanlee mentioned Charlie, and if she remembered him, and what he looked like, and what he said, etc. "If you do remember him and answer my questions, I'll give you another hundred which you don't have to split with the house."

"Can do."

Stanlee then helped her remember by describing Charlie and telling her how drunk he was.

Yvonne thought for a few seconds. "There was a cute guy, drunk as a skunk that I gave the works to, if you know what I mean. What else do you wanna know?"

"He told you a big story about jewels that he was going to inherit, bragging."

"Oh yeah, he said he was going to be rich and buy a hundred girls like me. He was really out of it."

"And he told you about a letter?"

"Yeah, I remember. He said his sister had it and was going to try to find all those jewels."

"By any chance, did he tell you where he lived?"

"Yeah, he was so drunk that he practically told me the story of his life."

"Did you tell anybody else about what Charlie said?"

She hesitated. "I think I told Mildred. She said drunks will say anything. Also, as we're told to do, I told Chen, one of Big Tan's henchmen. Big Tan is the boss of everything. We're told to pass on any information that they can use. I hate to say it, to blackmail people or get stock tips…stuff like that…I…can't believe I'm telling you all this!"

"Probably my charm," he said.

"In fact, maybe I told you too much. We're supposed to tell what we hear only to Chen or one of Big Tan's other employees. I hope you don't say anything. I talked too much. I don't want to get into any trouble."

"Don't worry. It's just between you and me. By the way, who's Chen?"

"I heard he's Big Tan's right-hand man. Who knows what he really does. I wouldn't want to find out."

"What's he look like?"

"He's a big guy, Chinese, also a muscular guy and almost as tall as you. From my experience and what the girls tell me, he'd make a good stud or porno star. He's got a real mean look about him, though. God knows, I wouldn't want to tangle with him!"

"Big Tan must be a really important person."

"Yeah, I heard he runs a lot of the massage parlors around here. They made him a lot of money. Also, the girls tell me he's in the drug-selling business as well as extorting business owners. I'd better shut up. I've said too much."

"No, I appreciate it. You've been very helpful." He handed her two more 50's.

"It's a shame, mister, that you got only talk for your 200 bucks. You sure you don't want anything else? Since you're such a generous guy, good-looking, too, I'll give you the works."

With that, she loosened the sash and her robe dropped to the floor, revealing her very shapely nude body. Stanlee thought he heard some shuffling and low voices outside the curtain, but he was so intent at looking at her naked body that nothing else mattered. For a moment of desire which he later denied to himself that he ever had, he almost forgot about Donna, his aversion to prostitutes, and his apparently rather flexible moral code.

Then, as the bamboo curtain was pushed aside, three men burst into the room and stood poised in what seemed to Stanlee to be like a melodramatic still scene from a motion picture. The man in the middle, who in Stanlee's perception seemed like a Cobra ready to strike, held a .45 automatic with silencer which he pointed at Yvonne.

"I told you, bitch, never to say anything that goes on here."

Yvonne, naked body shaking and with lips trembling, managed to eke out a few words. "I'm sorry, Chen. I don't know what got into me. I'm really sorry. It won't happen again."

"True. It's really a shame to waste such a beautiful body," he said calmly as his bullet pierced her temple.

Even in shock, Stanlee was still able to move toward her, but he stopped when Chen coldly said, “Don’t move.” In what seemed to Stanlee like slow motion, Chen turned the gun toward him and aimed it at his head.

Chapter 10
Murder

That afternoon the fickle weather replaced the sun with a light, drizzling rain which wasn't enough to deter Gaetano from meeting Guido at 2 pm. Perhaps they were getting paranoid since they suspected , without any proof, that somehow they were being watched (which they were) and perhaps being linked to the robbery of the swanky Rome jewelry store which was still a prominent news story in many major newspapers in Europe.

In a haunting scene which he would never forget as long as he lived, he heard frightening dialogue between Guido and two strangers. Just out of sight of the three men, Gaetano couldn't believe what he was hearing and seeing.

"Look you little shrimp. I'll ask you one more time." The dagger held by the man in the red cap was poised at Guido's throat. "Where are the diamonds and the rest of the jewels you stole - maybe with your friend you're always talking to?"

"What friend, mister? What are you talking about?"

"The one you talk to three or four times a day in the food line and out here. Don't lie to me. My friend and I have been observing you for a week since you got on board."

"Who the hell are you, "said the feisty Guido. "What do you want? I have no money."

"No, but you and your buddy somewhere have a fortune in jewels. It's none of your business who we are, but I'll tell you. Our boss at Vallone's hired us, private detectives, to follow you - the person who they thought was the number one suspect. You know the store, the people, the works. The store was robbed when you were on vacation. You somehow had a key made for the side door and the jewelry room and got the combination to the safe. They became even more suspicious when you wrote them a note telling them that you got another job and weren't coming back. A couple of the employees told the boss you were going to America pretty soon. We found out the name of the next ship going to America and got to the port in Naples just in time to check that you were on the manifest, and then we got on board."

"You're wasting your time. At the last minute I figured I had made enough money to go to America, which I always wanted to do, "said Guido, trying not to reveal his panic.

"Look, we know about you, dumbo with the big ears. The store employees said you were really smarter than you looked. Hard to believe!"

"Well, you wasted your money and your time. Do you think I could steal anything? Look at me. I was just a maintenance man."

"And a crook." The red-capped man pushed the dagger slightly harder into Guido's neck. "Look, you little pygmy, I'm going to shove this dagger right through your chicken neck if you don't tell us!" The tall man then laughed. "Your mother must have been a whore to give birth to such an ugly bastard like you!" Guido recoiled at the reference to his sainted mother, and his pent-up fear combined with anger exploded. "Go to hell you Italian jerk," Guido yelled and then spat in his face.

Without thinking of the consequences, the man in the red cap pushed the dagger into Guido's throat, splattering blood all over both of them. "Damn you!" Consumed with anger, he picked up Guido's dead body and with a burst of strength threw it, with the dagger still sticking in his throat, over the deck railing into the ocean.

"My God! What did you do! We'll never find the diamonds now. We'll never get the reward!" exclaimed his partner.

The killer, unknown to his partner, didn't care about the relatively small reward since he intended to escape with all the jewels and live a comfortable life in America - alone. "The hell with it. We'll find his friend. He probably has the jewels anyway and ..."

Before he could finish the sentence, Gaetano, wild-eyed and filled with rage, had sprung from his hiding place behind a partition intended to discourage or prevent immigrants from entering the garbage disposal area in the fantail. Gaetano, like a madman, threw his body across the two men who crashed against the railing. The smaller man, still dazed, started to get up, but before he could, Gaetano picked him up as if he were a rag doll and hurled him into the sea.

The man in the red cap looked at Gaetano who had just thrown his partner overboard and who looked big and strong enough to do the same to him. He started to run away, slipped on the rain-drenched deck, got up, and ran toward the nearest interior entrance.

Gaetano ran after him, skidded, and then stopped, realizing that he had dropped the satchel when he saw the horror of what happened to Guido. He went back, picked up the satchel, and walked unsteadily to his berth down below.

Still in shock, he sat down on the edge of his bed and cried. Was all this a nightmare? Did it really happen? His best friend was murdered! "Oh my God," he sobbed. "Oh my God." His body shook as he mentally replayed the ghostly scene of the dagger plunging into Guido's neck. He cried harder, murmuring "No, No, No." For a variety of reasons, many of the immigrants cried and out of respect for their anguish, the other immigrants pretended to hear and see nothing.

When he was able to control the trembling of his hands and stop the tears rolling down his cheeks, he forced himself to write, what he had previously intended to do, an explanatory and necessary letter to his brother, Vincenzo, in New York. He knew that a ship official would collect and safeguard all the letters and cards and deliver them safely to the U.S postal authorities after the passengers disembarked from the ship in a few days.

Gaetano, hands still shaking, began the letter that wouldn't be read by one of his descendants for almost a hundred years and would not only create a mystery, but would also be the cause of many other deaths.

The letter revealed his intention to somehow hide the jewels on Ellis Island to avoid confiscation in Customs if he couldn't for some reason get past the Inspectors.

"Dear Vincenzo"...

Chapter II
The Promise

Stanlee thought he had a couple of seconds to live after Chen killed the prostitute Yvonne and aimed the gun at his head. Suddenly Chen waved the .45 toward one of his companions and told him to "get rid of the bitch." Chen was now Big Tan's newly designated first assassin, and the boss' henchmen were afraid of him, his impatience, and violent nature when his orders were not quickly carried out.

"Turn around mister." Then Chen hit Stanlee hard on the back of his head with his gun. When Stanlee woke up, he tried to rub his eyes but couldn't because his hands were tied behind his back. As he looked around, he saw Chen, and apparently what must be Big Tan, and four of Tan's brawny bodyguards.

"Well, Mr. Stanlee, you finally woke up just as we took off the blindfold," said Tan. "You have some nice pictures in your wallet along with your Private Detective ID card."

"And you are?"

"Mr. Tan. But they call me Big Tan. And of course I know who you are thanks to what's in your wallet and what my spies here found out" (pointing to Chen and the four bodyguards).

Chen had to suppress laughing at the egotistical Tan who called himself "Big Tan" when the opposite was true. Chen looked at him as if he were looking at a pygmy with a pock-marked face and a hissing voice that would do justice to a rattlesnake.

Chen knew the answer about Tan's background, but he still couldn't believe how this short, ugly talentless man could still be so wealthy and powerful. The answer, of course, was that he inherited what he called "my Empire" from his father who had spent forty years building it up.

"Let me see, Mr. Stanlee. Steve, isn't it? Your father is David Stanlee who just retired as a police lieutenant working out of Manhattan South. I'm told we had a few run-ins with him when we tried to open up a couple of massage parlors in his district.

"Unlike some of his beat policemen, he couldn't be bribed. And he obviously didn't look the other way when we tried to extort money from some of the businessmen in his jurisdiction. He's lucky we didn't kill him. It would, however, have caused us too much trouble. Besides, we re-located about a mile away." There was no response from Stanlee.

Tan continued. "You're a graduate of Columbia College with high honors like your father… My congratulations for being such a good student," said Tan who was thrown out of primary school in Shanghai for what school administrators called "significant transgressions" which was a euphemism for stealing and also attempted rape.

"You've been a private detective, or what they call now a private investigator, for seven years, but officially for only three, and in such a short period of time you've been involved in some sensational cases, I might add. You renewed your two-year State license twice after you were officially certified at age 25. I see you paid your total license fee, $475, by certified check. As you can see, we also have sources in high places. As for your Mafia Cosa Nostra friend, 'the capo di tutti capi,' whose daughter you rescued, he won't help you. He's a business associate shall we say. He makes a fortune on the drugs we sell him."

"I see your thugs here really did their homework."

"They always do what I tell them," said Tan sternly. In his mind, Chen added "or else."

"Unfortunately, you are causing us some problems, and we can't afford your interference. You're in our way. If anybody can find the jewels, it'll be Chen."

Tan gave a signal to "Q" who then reached into his pocket and took out a long silk rope. Tan looked at Chen thinking that Chen possibly would have wanted to be the one to eliminate Stanlee since he was now the top assassin. But Tan, however, preferred the silence of the noose instead of the noise of a gunshot, with or without a silencer, or the blood from a dagger.

Suddenly, a vague memory crossed Chen's mind, and try as he could, he couldn't remember what it was until he saw "Q" smiling and approaching Stanlee as he wrapped part of a silk cord around one hand. "Wait a minute, 'Q.' The second assassin stopped for nobody when his boss gave an order, but something in

Chen's voice made him hesitate and look at Tan who said quietly, "Wait."

Chen remembered when he made his first promise ten years ago- a vow that was made before he left Shanghai and before he became an assassin so feared that he even frightened Tan's hoodlums, including the vicious "Q." In Stanlee he saw another private detective like Mr. Chang who ten years ago was so unbelievably kind to him and his parents. Somehow he linked the two men and remembered his resolve to help somebody the way Mr. Chang, who was like a second father to him, had generously aided him, his mother, and father.

Chen's father had often told him that "The gods of fate play strange tricks that can't be understood at the time." Bien said it when his son was plagued by some enormous problem (or so thought Chen) or some situation that was beyond his son's understanding. Did the so-called gods throw Stanlee in his path, thought Chen.

"I think, Big Tan (how he hated to call him by that ridiculous and inaccurate name), with due respect, I think we should let Stanlee help us find the so-called lost jewels. I know it's a small thing to you since you don't need the money, but it would be a challenge to see who finds them first. It would make things more exciting for me."

Tan looked at Chen quizzically. "If Stanlee finds the jewels," said Chen," he better make sure he doesn't lose his life doing so. If I find them, he loses the jewels, you get half, and I get half - or whatever you want."

Chen knew that Big Tan was a history buff who loved reading about Rome, and the early emperors, and how in a sense Tan considered himself an emperor. He particularly liked to read about the famous life-or-death individual combats in the Coliseum two thousand years ago. "It'll be like two gladiators fighting to the death and having the Emperor (he was going to add somebody like Caligula but thought that Tan might consider it an unfavorable reference) decide if the loser should live or die."

Tan interpreted Chen's implication that win or lose Stanlee would be the one getting the "thumbs down" or death. "OK, Chen, have your little game. We'll see who wins, if there is a winner. I owe you a couple of favors. It's the least I could do for my Number One Assassin."

Stanlee, who could hardly believe what he was hearing, relaxed, and his body stopped shaking involuntarily. "As long," added Chen, "Stanlee forgets about what happened in the Golden Palace or it's goodbye for him and his girlfriend. Understand, Stanlee?" Stanlee nodded "yes."

'Q,' said Tan, "blindfold him, and drop him off on 47th street where Peter picked him up."

Big Tan was amused and surprised at what Chen had proposed. But, he really didn't care about what happened to Chen or Stanlee, but it would be interesting to see how it would all end up. Maybe, "Q," was also thinking, Chen might be the loser, and he could once again be the Number 1 Assassin.

Chapter 12
Remembering Guido

In the middle of the night, Gaetano woke up after dreaming about Guido. How could it be that his friend of more than twenty years was gone and that he could never talk to him again, including their excited discussions about what they were going to do with all that money from the jewels to be sold in their new country? In the mixture of silence and the periodic noise of some immigrants talking and not sleeping, he imagined he heard the voice of Guido, from the other side of the hold, chattering away and laughing. But, it was only a delusion that Gaetano hoped was real, but it obviously wasn't.

His mind traveled back in time when two poor teenagers used to work in the orchards on the plains below Prizzi in order to make some money for their parents. He and Guido, with protective gloves provided by the owners, used to fill up baskets with the abundant cactus-prickly pears on the numerous trees and do the same with regular pears, oranges, lemons, peaches, and apples. The blackberries, blueberries, figs, grapes, olives, and strawberries were placed more delicately in smaller tray-like containers. The most difficult chore was plucking almonds and other nuts carefully from the many trees in the orchards.

They had preferred working in the convenient nearby orchards, just south of the winding dirt path leading to Prizzi, instead of the dirty and more difficult job tending to cattle, horses, and sheep enclosed behind wood fences on ranches two miles to the east.

The work of the men and teenagers was alertly monitored by guards, and sometimes owners, to safeguard against slackness, negligence, or particularly, stealing. In the past, some workers had either been fired for incompetence or prosecuted, for stealing usually in order to provide food, whether it be fruit, vegetables, berries or nuts, to feed their families for a few days.

Gaetano and Guido, except for a couple of times they raided the orchard when they were ten years old, were otherwise scrupulously honest because it was their teenage nature and because they didn't want to be exposed to the wrath of their upright and very religious Catholic parents. But, as adults, they soon came to realize that people on the verge of poverty and an uncertain future, sometimes resorted to desperate and dishonest measures.

Gaetano stopped thinking about Guido because he thought he was about to have another panic attack like the ones he had before the robbery on the way to join Guido in Rome. He had them on the 50 mile bus and train ride to Palermo, on the 20 mile ferry crossing from Palermo through the Strait of Messina to Naples, and worse ones on the 79 mile trip by train to Rome, where he happily joined Guido.

From Rome he had gone by bus with Guido back to Naples. In Naples, he and Guido, before paying $35 each for a steerage ticket, were given a cursory physical examination, vaccination, and then required to answer questions on a form filed for the record by the transport company. In routine procedures, visas had to be obtained from the American Consul in Naples and also from the Italian government.

There were three Italian ports where Italian immigrants in 1913 could board immigrant ships bound for America: Genoa, Naples, and Palermo, capital of Sicily. Naples was a more convenient choice for them because it was nearer Rome and could save them time instead of making the unnecessary trip back to Sicily.

It took awhile but Gaetano fell asleep and started again to dream.

Chapter 13
Chen's Father

Bien Chen tried to give his son all the advantages he didn't have as a young man growing up in Shanghai. In listening to his father's stories, Chen developed even more respect for him when he realized the hardship his father had endured and his struggle to earn enough money to enter the famed Fudan University and later to support his family. As Bien hoped would also later happen to Peter, he was awarded a college scholarship on the condition that he maintained satisfactory grades each semester.

What Bien didn't tell Peter was that for most of his teenage years, he helped pay for his parents' subsistence and for all his future college expenses by working for the notorious mobster, Big Tan. Bien, at that time, didn't comprehend that he was entering what would be a life of crime for decades and not just a short-term job to earn money. Bien, for years, by sea had delivered a variety of narcotics to wholesalers and retailers, as well as to well-to-do individuals, who were in towns bordering the East China and South China Seas.

At first, he was accompanied by a drug trafficking veteran, but eventually he learned to be independent and how to maneuver the sampans by himself. But the oar-driven, flat-bottomed skiffs were soon considered to be too slow, and so they eventually were replaced by speedier motorboats and cabin cruisers. Peter sometimes wondered how his science-oriented father was so knowledgeable about boats and the towns bordering both seas.

His father eventually told Peter how he so impressed his immediate supervisors that they recommended to Big Tan that he be transferred to the main drug laboratory located in Shanghai. Bien happily considered it a promotion because of the higher salary and not having to contend with the long hours, the sea's bad weather, and the annoying complaints of some of Big Tan's customers.

When he graduated from Fudan University with high honors and obtained a position there as a college instructor of Chemistry and Physics, he was soon promoted to be Tan's Chief of Laboratory Services, replacing the man who had just died. The job was part-time and required Bien to work almost at his convenience, usually only when large drug shipments arrived. When Bien told his wife about his new, much higher salary, she was ecstatic. The two combined salaries would move them a notch above Middle Class.

Peter, however, later became aware that his father would not have continued to work for Big Tan if he didn't need the money for an improved life style for him and his mother. Through the years, his father had complained to his wife about Big Tan's rudeness and insulting nature and his reputation for hiring assassins to kill people he didn't like or who infringed in any way on his business empire. His mother reluctantly once told him, "Sometimes, Peter, you have to do things you don't want to." This bit of advice much later sustained him through some difficult times.

Peter sometimes wanted to see what Big Tan looked like and determine if his father's description of him was on the mark: a small, thin man with "cruel eyes" and a pock-marked face regarded as ugly if anyone was foolish or daring enough to say so. Big Tan destroyed men and women, for lesser insults or transgressions.

Peter had cringed about the widely circulated rumor that Big Tan had one of his assassins, called "Q," murder his wife, Shi, by strangling her with his trademark silk noose. After she had married him, apparently for his money and certainly not for his appearance or personality, she became dissatisfied. Unfortunately, her comments to her father, a successful regional drug dealer, were overheard by one of Big Tan's hoodlums. "Father, she said, "he's so ugly and boring, and he's impotent most of the time."

Bien had never told the young Peter that Big Tan had criticized and humiliated him frequently even in front of his subordinate lab assistants. He told his wife who agreed with him that he couldn't quit until they paid off a lot of debts, including anticipated college tuition for Peter. Big Tan had a reputation for not allowing some of his key subordinates to quit or even retire if they were important contributors to the welfare of his drug, prostitution, and extortion businesses.

Peter once asked his father how his boss got the name "Big Tan" and why he wasn't always in Shanghai. Bien laughed. "He's a very small, thin and quite ugly man, and to boost his ego he ordered his gang members to call him 'Big Tan' or else. I guess he had an inferiority complex and tried to compensate for it. A very foolish and disturbed, dangerous man." "Of course," his father would add after his harangue about Tan, "he would be a nobody today if his father hadn't built up the business and left it to him after he died."

Bien added that Big Tan now lived mostly in his mansion in Westchester County in New York and flew to Shanghai five or six times a year to check on the Shanghai branch of his business. Employees dreaded his visits to Shanghai because he was known to fire an employee for the most insignificant reason-or sometimes have him eliminated.

The only time Bien said something positive about Big Tan occurred when he discussed Tan's Afghanistan venture. "It was the only thing he did that his father didn't start," said Bien. Years ago Tan bought acres of land there and hired the locals to grow and process the deceptively lovely poppy plants before shipping the crop to his warehouse in Shanghai.

The poppies were the source of opium, the best selling narcotic not only in Shanghai but in other parts of China. Outside of Shanghai, however, the authorities frowned on the opium trade despite its popularity. As his scientifically-oriented father would say, "Poppies are pretty but deadly flowers and capsular fruits with one, somniferum, containing the source of opium. They've unfortunately ruined many lives."

Big Tan lately had worried about his diminishing investment in Afghanistan where the government and coalition troops were ordered to destroy as many poppy fields as possible. As a result, many independent farmers were ruined, but Tan's generous bribes and influence kept him in business. Tan, however, had confided to his Afghanistan supervisors, that if his poppy fields were destroyed, he would replace them with the in-demand wheat grain or corn or both.

It was no surprise that Peter came to dislike Big Tan whom he had never met and actually didn't want to. But, the lives of Big Tan and Peter would soon be intertwined in a way that neither could have ever imagined.

Chapter 14
Shanghai

Peter's father had regarded Peter as someone special since he was a child who had impressed his primary school teachers with his intelligence and ability to easily retain knowledge. As his son grew older, Bien Chen realized that his son also was very ambitious and exhibited a determination to excel in anything that he tried to do. Bien, hardly reaching 5 feet, 6 inches tall, marveled at the source of the genes which added another six inches to his son's height.

For a while, Bien whimsically wondered if Peter might have been touched by the "ancient gods of fate" who gave him height, good looks, intelligence, and a charismatic personality. But what worried him most was his son's promiscuity-his preoccupation with sex. Peter progressed from having numerous amorous dalliances with teenage girlfriends and then equally frequent liaisons with older women, including bar girls, many of whom were professional prostitutes - all before Peter was eighteen years old.

On his eighteenth birthday, his parents surprised him with something he had previously been hinting about-an expensive Sony computer and Canon printer. "Now, you can type your college papers on this brand new computer," his father said. Peter was careful to show his father the proper respect and appreciation for such an expensive gift. "Xiexie." (thank you) said Peter, and Bien responded with "bukegi" (you're welcome).

His father didn't know it, but Peter had no intention of attending college in Shanghai or anywhere else. He was planning to tell his parents that, with the money that he had saved from part-time jobs, he was going to the United States to seek a different life and take advantage of the many unique and exciting opportunities there.

His father would have been very disappointed since he had helped expedite arranging for a four- year scholarship for Peter at the famous and exclusive Fudan University where for many years Bien was a professor of Chemistry and Physics. Bien had his son visit him several times at the university on Handan Road so he could get a view of the expansive campus and a brief taste of university life.

His father had been worried that in the past two years Peter had been too attracted to Shanghai's night life, including the attractive women who either worked in or frequented the many teahouses (which were losing ground to the more exotic establishments), night clubs, restaurants, and bars where young people, mostly 18 to 30, socialized. Customers in these establishments frequently gravitated to small rooms, conveniently furnished with small beds, and hidden with either opaque lace or bamboo curtains. Fortunately, Peter always carried a package of condoms in his wallet-a fact unknown to his conservative and old-fashioned parents.

Bien knew that Peter in the warm weather also liked to impress young ladies with mini-picnics by the lake on the lush green grass in the middle of a circle of rose bushes and ginkgo trees in the heart of the beautiful Ding Xiang Gardens. The ginkgo trees not only provided privacy but also shade.

He always brought small sandwiches, traditional picnic fruit (oranges or watermelon), oolong tea (a mixture of black and green teas), and dessert (either Babaofan, which was a sweet rice pudding, warm buns, or other pastries with cream fillings). At first, his mother helped prepare the picnic basket for his "little girlfriends," but eventually he assumed the task himself, especially when his "girlfriends" were not so little and sometimes delighted in sexually experimenting. Once he entertained an English lady, a tourist, who was curious about the name of the city, Shanghai, and the term "shanghaied." He explained a little of the notorious history of the city and also that, a long time ago, ruthless men supplied crewmen for ships departing from Shanghai to other ports in the Orient as well as to those all over the world.

For a generous fee per person, the hired thugs would drag or carry drunk or opium-drugged men to the many ships docked in the harbor. When the "shanghaied" or kidnapped men awoke from their stupor, they were given two choices - work as a seaman for the duration of the trip or be thrown overboard. Since the ship was usually miles from shore, they elected the obvious choice.

For this intriguing tale as well as others, plus her lustful mood, desire, and her physical attraction to Peter, and a large glass of the hot and alcohol-laden sake, the English lady, nicknamed Jig, happily took off all of her clothes. In the approaching dusk, Peter later told his friends, he had the sexual time of his life with a nude, drunk, and almost insatiable tiger of a woman.

Chapter 15
Tan's Revenge

Peter's father, now 74, decided to retire at the risk of possibly incurring the wrath of Big Tan. Bien mistakenly assumed that Big Tan, as a reward for his many years of dedicated service, would not oppose his retirement. But he was wrong. Despite Big Tan's rants and threats in a personal meeting, Bien was firm in his decision to retire not only from his college job but also from Big Tan's employ.

Big Tan carried through on his threats. He strong-armed Bien's creditors to have them demand immediate payment of Bien's debts. A couple of Big Tan's underlings waylaid Bien as he was unlocking his front door. Since they knew and liked Bien, they complied with Big Tan's orders but only half-heartedly hit Bien on the head with a short club and then pushed him against his front door. "Sorry, Bien," said one of them. "We had to give you a warning as Big Tan wanted. You know how he is."

A year later, the Chen's had no choice but to move to a cheaper house in a poorer section in the southeast fringes of the city near the East China Sea. Bien's modest college retirement income was not enough to cover current expenses and to pay off remaining past debts. What concerned father and son most, however, was the sudden illness of Peter's mother, Jiang, who was diagnosed as having breast cancer. Bien tried to keep up with the medical expenses but made little progress. The two men had to accept whatever jobs they could find to pay the medical and other bills.

If it weren't for one man, Mr. Zhu Chang, the Chen's would have faced inevitable financial disaster. After a casual conversation between Bien and Mr. Chang who met in a local supermarket, they became good friends. Zhu Chang was a retired Shanghai police officer who, out of boredom in retirement, became a private detective. Mr. Chang soon realized the financial plight of the family who, for lack of money, ran out of food in the last 3 or 4 days of the month. He would always arrive in the last week of the month with baskets of food and a bottle of wine. The Chen's would mildly protest each time, but they had to respect the ancient Chinese tradition of not rejecting gifts of a good friend.

Even though Zhu Chang lived a half mile away in a more respectable and expensive neighborhood, he never boasted or lost his humble and compassionate nature. Mr. Chang was also careful not to bring chili, once a favorite of Peter's, since he knew that Peter despised it after having to eat the inexpensive chili seven or eight times a month. Peter loved to hear stories of Shanghai criminals which Mr. Chang colorfully told. Zhu Chang liked the amiable and respectful Peter who he thought was an intelligent and inquisitive young man.

Peter later admitted to his good friend Kimmie that Mr. Chang became like a second father to him. He vowed that someday he would emulate him and try to help someone in need as Mr. Chang had helped him and his parents. Peter couldn't know that the first of his two sacred vows would be tested under dramatic conditions years later.

Peter thought that Mr. Chang reminded him of Kimmie who also was a very kind and generous soul. Thomas Kim was studying architecture at Fudan University. It was difficult to see his friend as much as he used to since Kim was a busy student in the prestigious college located in the northeastern outskirts of Shanghai. Unlike his other friends who had deserted him after Big Tan harassed and ruined his father, Kimmie was always loyal and would visit Peter as often as he could.

Kimmie was now the only young person who socialized with Chen and also kept the secret that his friend's dream was to live in America with its promises of opportunities. That very weekend, Kimmie invited him to dinner at one of Peter's favorite Hunanese restaurants, Di Shui Dong. Peter loved its rural ambience and its excellent food, especially the fried chicken and spare ribs followed by one of his favorite desserts, the tasty caramelized bananas. Kimmie didn't mention what Peter used to order, Lazi Jiding, which was fried chicken combined with steaming hot chili since he knew why Peter now disliked chili.

The evening reminded Chen of what he used to take for granted - a lifestyle of fun, drinking, eating at the best restaurants, and picking out oriental beauties for what he called sexual "fun time." Kim paid for the meal, despite Peter's mild but respectful objection. As Kim drove Peter home, in his old 2001 dark green Buick LeSabre, now a discontinued model, the subject of the United States came up again.

"You know, Kimmie, if I ever get to the United States, it would be great if you could come over, too."

"Could be Peter, but I like it here in Shanghai though tourists call it 'sin city' and 'the city with all the vices.'"

"They don't really know and understand Shanghai the way we do. It really is a fantastic place."

"True," said Kimmie, "So why don't you stay?"

"There are a lot of different opportunities in America, as I always told you… jobs, women, adventure…"

"Especially women. Sometimes, Peter, I think you're addicted to sex and women."

"There could be worst things, Kim old buddy. Come with me. It'll be an adventure!"

"No I can't. Besides I met this girl…"

"You're kidding." Chen never associated the slender, black-haired shy Kim and his large eyeglasses with a girlfriend.

"Is it serious?"

"You bet, Peter. She's very sweet, very pretty, and in some of my classes."

"Amazing, Kim, with a girlfriend. I hope she's not a call girl!"

You know better. Quit kidding, Peter, it's serious."

Peter remembered what he and his former friends had arranged for Kim on his sixteenth birthday. They wanted their obviously virgin friend to be introduced to the world of sex. They all chipped in and paid a lovely and scantily clad bar girl (some doubled serving drinks and later providing sex) to flirt with Kim and then bring him next door to the Ultra Asian Palace Hotel. The dimly-lit room, which they paid for in advance, featured an extra large bed and colorful replicas of famous salacious Chinese paintings.

Chen knew the hotel manager, who hadn't seen one of his best and youngest customers in a long time, and who gave Peter a generous discount "for old time's sake" but actually because business was slow. Chen was attracted to this hotel where he brought many of his girlfriends because of its 1930's old-style architecture where he could imagine he lived in the fantasy of a bygone era.

Peter interrupted his reverie to ask Kim what his girlfriend's name was.

"Tang Wei."

"Nice name. How old is she?"

"Eighteen, like me."

"Kind of young, don't you think?"

"I don't think so Peter. We're the same age. She's sophisticated, very smart, very pretty, and very wholesome."

"I don't know about the wholesome part."

"Cool it, Peter. You're always thinking about sex."

"Not really."

"She's just about the best thing that ever happened to me. We met in one of our English classes. English 2, of all places."

"Why do you say that, Kim?"

"Well, if you ever convinced me to go to the United States, I'd have a head start speaking the English language."

"Good thinking."

Chen, not now used to late hours, said, "I have to get some sleep, Kim. Thanks for a great time and paying for the dinner. Zai Jian."

"Bye, Peter. I'll call you next week. Maybe I'll come over so you can meet her."

"Fine, if we still have a phone. I don't know if the bill was paid. Things aren't what they used to be, Kim."

"I know. I know. See ya."

As Chen walked down the short dirt path, he noticed that there was no light on in his house. One of his father's habits was to leave at least one light on overnight. When he saw the front door open and unlocked, he became alarmed. Chen knew that people here in this poor section who had nothing tried to steal something from their neighbors who also had nothing. A crazy situation.

Peter first looked in his parents' bedroom where they should have been at this late hour. Growing increasingly anxious, he looked for a weapon of some sort but couldn't find one. Thinking he could get a knife from one of the drawers in the kitchen, he moved cautiously and slowly into the kitchen and flicked the light switch and almost fainted as he stared at the most horrible sight in his young life.

Chapter 16
Horror

For a few seconds, Chen was in shock - what he saw seemed worse than a surreal nightmare. In his panic he didn't know what to do-yell, scream, cry. As he fell to his knees, he let out a piercing cry that would have frightened even him if he weren't intensely and obliviously staring at his dead father, Bien, and mother, Jiang, who just a few hours ago were joking with him about his latest girlfriend.

In disbelief, he saw that around their necks was an indentation that could only be the mark of some kind of rope or cord which the killer must have used to strangle them. Chen, after he had stopped sobbing and calmed down, noticed that his father also had a deep bruise on his forehead.

Shanghai homicide detectives, arrived after being called by Mr. Chang, who had responded to Peter's frantic, almost unintelligible phone call, and who believed the contusion on Bien's forehead was made by some blunt instrument. Out of respect for Chang, their former colleague, the detectives had accompanied two Shanghai police officers officially sent to investigate. Peter, even in his anguish, verbally expressed his appreciation for Chang's help and comforting presence.

In the interrogation by the detectives, Chen deliberately left out relevant and important information. He remembered what his father had told him about Qui, known to his fellow mobsters as "Q." "Q" reputedly was Big Tan's Number One Assassin whose favorite method of killing was to strangle his victims with a thick silk rope. Only behind "Q's" back and not within earshot would his fellow thugs call him Ysheng (Doctor) Death or Shan (mountain) because of his nasty temper and intimidating 6-5 height and weight, almost 300 pounds.

It was rumored, which Chen's father said was really fact, that "Q" had killed more than 100 people, including women. Some of the victims were Big Tan's dispensable competitors in the drug trade. Other victims included Big Tan's first and only wife, Shi, who grew tired of him and vice-versa, and women, mostly prostitutes, who made the fatal mistake of laughing at Tan or spurning his sometimes impotent sexual efforts.

People couldn't believe, or didn't want to believe, that Big Tan had "Q" strangle his wife. Big Tan had met the flirtatious Shi several years ago when he traveled to the Fujian province in southeastern China to try to resolve a dispute regarding discounts with Shi's father, one of his biggest drug wholesalers in southern China. At a dinner party given by Shi's father in Tan's honor, Shi saw wealth, prestige, and a large inheritance if she married, as she later said, this "unpleasant ugly old worm." The gossip abounded why such a beautiful woman would marry Tan, who at 60, was more than three times her age.

After a year of marriage, he tired of her, especially when he had many mistresses at his constant disposal who loved his money so much that they overlooked his ugliness, mean temper, and frequent impotence. The rumor was that Big Tan without remorse ordered "Q" to strangle his wife after she departed Shanghai (where she resided most of the time) to visit her parents in their palatial home in the Fujian province.

For many months later, Chen thought frequently about Big Tan and "Q" and vowed that he would somehow keep what he called his "sacred" promise to avenge the death of his parents. Since his former friends had deserted him after his father was ruined by Big Tan, the only person who observed that Peter Chen's attitude and behavior had drastically changed was his friend, Kimmie. The carefree, jovial, compassionate, hedonistic Peter Chen seemed to metamorphose, except toward Kim, into a more serious, cold, and anti-social person.

But, with Kim, Peter continued to be as friendly and sociable as he previously had been with his best friend. If Thomas Kim, however, could see the obsession overwhelming his friend, he would have been terribly worried.

With the little money he had saved and what little was left of his parents' funds, he bought a one-way ticket from Pudong International Airport in Shanghai to John F. Kennedy Airport in New York City. Kim, who had driven Peter to the airport to see him embark, would never in a million years have guessed Peter's specific future deadly intentions.

In New York City, Peter planned to convince Big Tan, who had never seen the son of his former chief chemist, to hire him as an assassin or a bodyguard or in some other capacity as long as he remained close to Big Tan. His knowledge of

Big Tan's empire and other details of his criminal activities was the accumulated result of listening to hundreds of stories told to him by his father over the years. In case he was hired as an assassin, he had paid a local minor hoodlum to teach him about guns, silencers, and the use of daggers.

Chen planned to work for Big Tan for a reasonable length of time during which he would make enough money to return to Shanghai and lead an even more luxurious life than he used to have. And, of course, all of this would happen after he kept his promise of getting revenge for the murder of his parents. When his parental vow was kept, he would immediately return to Shanghai. But, he didn't know that he would remain in America for ten years before he would face the greatest challenge of his life.

Chapter 17
Return to Shanghai

Nine years later, after he graduated from the elite Fudan University, and married his college sweetheart, Thomas Kim had finally accepted Chen's advice and pleas to join him in the United States, specifically New York City. The city, Chen wrote, was much less dangerous and crime-filled than Shanghai.

Chen had gone out of his way to convince his only true friend to come to America. Chen truly appreciated that Kimmie hadn't deserted him after his father was ruined financially and after he and his parents were forced to move to a less than desirable section just south of Fuz Hou Road near the Huangpu River in Shanghai.

Kimmie and his wife and Peter usually had bi-weekly get-togethers in various New York City Chinese restaurants. Chen liked to have lunch with Kimmie and his wife, Tang. Their favorite Chinatown restaurant, New Shanghai Cousin, was similar in decor and menu to its counterpart in Shanghai. The trio liked this particular Chinatown bistro because it was a combination restaurant and night club and also featured food they were accustomed to in Shanghai. They had a variety of dishes to choose from: smoked fish, crabs, sushi, garlic veal, in addition to other meals and a variety of Chinese and Japanese wines.

Unlike his two friends, Chen got accustomed to using utensils and not chopsticks. In fact, in China, Chen had difficulty holding the two thin round-tipped chopsticks between his thumb and his other fingers. His father used to chide him about not being Chinese enough.

Kimmie didn't know what Chen had secretly done for him in addition to paying for airline tickets from Pudong International Airport to Kennedy Airport, which was located in southeast New York City.

With copious amounts of drugs he had personally removed, without question, from Tan's primary New York City warehouse, he bribed the owner of an apartment building near Chinatown to rent very cheaply a deluxe suite to Kim. Also, the head of a prestigious architectural firm would hire anyone Chen wanted as long as the free supply of marijuana and cocaine and whatever else he wanted, was delivered to him regularly. None of Tan's warehouse workers, threatened by Chen, would dare tell Tan what his chief assassin, a very dangerous man, took from his warehouse.

As dessert arrived, Kim and Chen were both reluctant to tell what each thought was bad news. Actually it was good news since they were all planning to return to Shanghai.

"Peter, it's hard for me to tell you, after all you've done for us, but we're going back home, to Shanghai."

"You're kidding! I was just going to tell you the same thing. I've saved enough money, and after a few days taking care of some details, I'm flying back."

"We booked a flight Monday morning from Kennedy to Pudong International Airport," said Kim.

"I'll probably leave about a week or so after you," said Chen.

"Will you be staying at your parents' house, Kimmie?"

"Yeah, until we get a place of our own. First thing when you get in, come over."

"Will do, Kimmie. Do you have a job lined up there?"

"I got a lead on an architect's job there. My boss here told me about it. He was very helpful."

"And Tang."

"She was once offered a job teaching math at the university. She's going to see if it's still available."

As they ate the caramelized bananas, Chen said, "Do you remember we used to have this dessert in…"

"In Di Shui Dong restaurant on South Shanxi Road. It was one of your favorite desserts. You liked the place which served one of your favorite dinners-chili and fried chicken."

"True, but as you know, I lost my taste for chili a long time ago."

Like many Shanghaiese, they could never get enough of the variety of foods they were again looking forward to in the hundreds of eating places in Shanghai, a Chinese city of almost fourteen million people.

As the check arrived which Chen always took care of, Kimmie's wife asked Chen

"Are you getting a job in Shanghai working for Tan?"

"I think I'll try to get involved in a piece of Tan's empire or go into business myself."

"What kind of empire, Peter?"

Knowing that Kimmie's wife was oblivious of his job as an assassin, Chen said, "Oh, it's something in imports." Chen and Kimmie looked at each other and hoped that she wouldn't ask any more questions.

"Before we leave, Peter, I'd like to thank you again for the two-week job you gave me. It'll pay for most of the airfare."

Chen had hired Kimmie to follow Stanlee and use an electronic device to record his conversation, especially when he was with his girlfriend, Donna.

"When did you say you're flying back, Kimmie?"

"Monday morning. An 11 am flight from Kennedy to Pudong Airport."

"That's a long airplane ride. I'll call you this Friday or Saturday night, before you leave, old buddy."

The two men, friends since childhood, were still overjoyed at the prospect of eventually being reunited in the city where they had grown up. Kimmie had eventually adjusted to the fact that his best friend had become an assassin. Chen walked to his car and waved, knowing that there was a good chance that if his plans didn't succeed, he would never see them again.

Chapter 18
Ellis Island

Along with almost 2000 other immigrants, mostly from southern European countries, particularly Italy and Sicily, Gaetano waited on one of the three decks.

The immigrant ship, formerly used for a brief time to transport commercial cargo instead of human beings, moved into Upper New York Bay after navigating through the Narrows between Brooklyn and Staten Island. Gaetano, like most of the other prospective Americans, exhibited alternating emotions of fear, joy, and hopeful expectation.

As the ship neared the New York City port on the southern tip of Manhattan, the crowd became relatively silent. Not very far from Ellis Island, the grandeur of the Statue of Liberty on Bedloe's Island came into view. The crowd cheered, yelled, and watched in amazement as the ship moved past Bedloe's Island, almost a mile south of Ellis Island.

Adding to the wonder was the astonishing sight of almost unbelievably tall buildings forming the Manhattan skyline. Dominating the sight was the recently completed 60-story Woolworth Building which, in 1913, was considered to be an architectural marvel. Gaetano, unable to contain his emotions, wept at the sight of the American shoreline, and then pushed his luggage - a large suitcase and a strapless satchel with handle - closer to him. Someone next to him said that they were heading either for the port at Hoboken, New Jersey, or as it turned out, the pier at the lower end of Manhattan.

It was apparent that the cabin passengers, who paid a much higher price for their tickets, would disembark before the steerage immigrants who paid only $35 for a one-way ticket which paid for only inferior accommodations. After the ship docked, it took a long time for the immigrants to disembark and be led to wharves where barges would ferry them to Ellis Island.

The first class cabin passengers, because of the much higher price they paid, had the privilege of being processed on board ship and allowed to head for their American destinations without being detained at Ellis Island. Needless to say, usually the extra cabin charge they paid, sometimes with an additional bribe, hastened their entry into the country. If Gaetano and Guido had the money, they certainly would have preferred the luxury of crossing the ocean in a deluxe cabin. They knew that they couldn't get any money from selling the jewels until they realized their long-term ambition and were in America.

In deference to ships entering the harbor, the immigrants, or "aliens" as some disrespectful dock workers referred to them, had to wait an unusually long time to board the barges. While waiting, Gaetano kept looking nervously around as if he were looking for someone who may have been watching him. As the immigrants became more impatient and started noisily grumbling and verbally complaining, the guide from Ellis Island said, "Be patient, a couple of more ships are almost docked, and then we can board the barges."

As the immigrants continued to wait on the wharves, vendors, some not very honest, yelled out inflated prices for various food items. Gaetano had some Italian money (lire) left even though he had used some of it to pay a kind old Sicilian lady to twice wash his clothes on the two-week voyage. On sale were cakes, usually stale, and fruits and vegetables which were sold at outrageous prices - usually two or three times higher than the usual city price. Gaetano fingered the few remaining Italian coins he had in his pocket and bought a green apple with a silver coin which the seller accepted and would exchange later in a bank for American money.

Gaetano looked down at the badge marked "B2O" which was pinned to the chest area of his jacket. The tag, with a letter and number, corresponded to the ship's passenger form, or manifest, which had room for only 30 names. Handwritten on each of the large cardboard forms was the passenger's name, height, weight, date of birth, and birthplace. Everyone was required to wear the tag, including children. At the point of embarkation in Naples, before boarding ship, the tags were given to passengers for identification purposes.

The tag reminded him of his mother who had pinned his name and address on a piece of paper on his first day of primary school in Prizzi. As reminders of his late parents, he had several pictures of them in the large suitcase. He thought also of the treasured gift his mother gave him on one of his late teenage birthdays-a small carpenter's tool box which contained a small hammer, chisel, a few other tools plus a tube containing a paste-like adhesive. She knew that Gaetano had always liked carpentry work. The pictures and toolbox were the only reminders of his parents that he had room for in his large suitcase.

Finally, amid sighs of relief, orders were given to board the long barges which could each accommodate not more than about 200 passengers. The barges, similar to medium-sized cruise ships, had a large enclosure in its middle with rows of wooden benches inside. The barges had fragile-looking low wood railings on its sides. In good weather, many of the immigrants stood on the deck looking out at the Hudson River and searching for their first glimpse of Ellis Island.

In the early 1890's, for a very short time, the government, in good weather, used flat-bottomed open boats originally used for carrying commercial cargo in inland waterways. But these vessels without rails were very quickly abandoned since they obviously were too impractical and dangerous in any kind of weather.

In 1913, the more recent large barges, which had smokestacks issuing much smoke, had the words "Department of Commerce and Labor" and "U.S. immigration Service" clearly marked on each side.

Gaetano was still awed by the sights of the Statue of Liberty and the Manhattan skyline which were his first glimpses of America and expectantly waited for his first view of Ellis Island.

The barge ships moved slowly, trailing each other, as they crossed the Hudson River, toward Ellis Island which was located west of Governor's Island and north of Bedloe's Island (now renamed Liberty Island) where stood the impressive Statue of Liberty. Ellis Island was named after businessman Samuel Ellis who unsuccessfully tried to sell the island in 1785 by advertising it as "Oyster Island" which he thought was a more colorful and appealing name to potential buyers.

During the short voyage, lasting almost an hour, Gaetano fought off nausea as he thought of the possibility of rejection at the threshold of entering the United States and/or his inability to safely hide the jewels on Ellis Island. And he kept thinking about his dear friend Guido whom he wished was there with him. Many times, in the past few days, he had sobbed thinking about Guido and how excited he would also have been seeing Ellis Island.

Outside, with two pieces of luggage in hand and feeling nauseous, he pushed his way past other passengers on the large deck. He leaned over the low railing and vomited. He hardly heard one of the crewmen yelling, "Get away from there! You want to die! You could end up in the river!"

Chapter 19
The Clues

In the kitchen of his four-room apartment in Massapequa, Stanlee read the letter at least a dozen times. Frustrated, after three hours of analyzing the letter, he poured a third glass of Burgundy wine. Three glasses of the dark wine wouldn't bother him, but two more and he would be finished for the night.

"Five" he said, softly, "five. Of course! That must be it. God, what else could it be! It's really very simple." He read the letter again and everything suddenly clicked into place. He understood the implied message. His admiration increased for Gaetano who must have been a very clever man!

He said loudly the key words that he had put together: "chisel…read this letter carefully…find the jewels…go to the washroom… five times…five…the Reception Center…five times…five days…Ellis Island."

Stanlee combined the words into sentences that Gaetano expected his brother hopefully would have figured out if Gaetano, for some reason, didn't get through Customs or didn't survive. *"Read this letter carefully. Go to number 5 Washroom in the Reception Center on Ellis Island. Use a chisel to find the jewels. Good luck."*

Even though it was almost three in the morning, he had to telephone Donna. She was very excited when he told her the promising news. He also told her that in three days, on Friday, he would go to Ellis Island after he asked his father for two favors: arranging for transportation to Ellis Island and authorization to permit his unimpeded investigation there. Knowing how efficient his father was, he expected him somehow to arrange for the boat ride from the southern tip of Manhattan to Ellis Island and to secure the permit in one or two days.

At breakfast tomorrow (8 am sharp), he would tell Donna about the clues in the letter and also review his plans to be on Ellis Island Friday afternoon. Little did he know that at Matty's Breakfast House on Long Beach Road in Oceanside, a black-haired, spectacled young man would unobtrusively be listening to and recording their conversation.

Chapter 20
Hiding the Jewels

Finally arriving at Ellis Island, the still nauseous Gaetano was herded with the others to an area just beyond the quay. At this landing place, interpreters barked out directions, in various languages, to follow them to the main buildings. The buildings consisted mainly of a large Reception Center with room for luggage in the front, a medical center, boiler room, laundry room, an electrical supply area, and some other utility areas.

"More walking," complained Gaetano to himself as he looked to his right and imagined that Guido was there beside him. Even though the cheerful Guido wasn't with him now, his memory comforted and inspired him.

In the spacious Reception Center, he put down his tagged large suitcase but not his satchel. For an immigrant who may have been used to living in little rooms, like Gaetano, the entrance hall was gigantic. It was more than 150 yards long and 70 feet wide. Unlike the outside of the building which was built with brick, cement, and iron, the hall inside was constructed only with wood and iron beams. There were wood benches past the guarded luggage area and then a series of aisles leading to the Customs Inspectors.

In small groups, the immigrants were first directed to climb one of the two side staircases leading to a balcony which encircled the hall. In a series of rooms at the top, doctors or medical aides checked each immigrant's skin, eyes, mouth, and anything else that looked suspicious or unhealthy. Those with significant problems were directed to a special room to undergo more stringent tests. Those passing the battery of tests would go downstairs to the main floor via one of the staircases on each side of the balcony.

After waiting his turn for twenty minutes on the right or east side of the balcony,

Gaetano asked for permission from one of the attendants to use the lavatory. On the way to the two lavatories at the north end of the hall, it was fortunate that he didn't understand English when one of the guards said, "All these foreigners stink and are dirty. I wonder when the last time was that they had a bath. I hate to go near them."

The other guard was more sympathetic. "Look, if you spent two weeks in the hold of an immigrant ship, you'd look and smell lousy. I know. My uncle, who came over from Florence three years ago, said the living conditions were horrible." Then he went into more detail about what he meant by "horrible."

Gaetano was pleasantly surprised when he saw that Washroom #5 was marked "MEN" and #6 "WOMEN." Apparently Americans, for modesty's sake, separated the two genders. After he finished urinating, he examined the floors and ceiling of the male Washroom.

After returning to his place in line, he wondered what questions on the main floor the Customs Inspector, the last hurdle to overcome in order to enter the United States, would ask. According to rumor, the questions were generally about an immigrant's name, as listed on the ship's manifest, occupation, money at hand, destination in America, and any discernible negative aspects of one's background. What had originally worried Gaetano and Guido was that the Inspector, in checking luggage and clothing, would find and confiscate the jewels and have them detained and ultimately sent back to Sicily where they certainly would be faced with the prospect of prison. But that would not now be a problem if he were able to follow his plan to hide the jewels in a safe place-in a location that Guido told him about in discussing the layout of the building.

Gaetano, after passing the series of tests, and as he had planned, went back to the men's Washroom #5 further down on the balcony, holding his heavy satchel. On his way, he saw a pretty young woman, apparently Italian and about 20 or 21. She smiled at him, and for the first time in many months, romantic and sexual urges temporarily blanked out his anxiety and fear. Perhaps if she were still there later, he would dare to approach her.

In the Men's Washroom, he locked the door to the stall and put down his satchel. Before he took out the small hammer, chisel, screwdriver, and small tube containing an adhesive, he again examined the walls and the floor. He started to sweat as he tried to determine a safe and not easily observable place to hide the jewel-laden satchel. What would he do if there was no way to hide them!

Suddenly the location of the hiding place seemed obvious to him-behind and below the commode. Who would look there, and if he did, Gaetano believed he would camouflage the area so well that it would be virtually impossible to detect that the cement block in question had been disturbed.

He kneeled, and with the hammer he gently tapped the chisel around the edges of a mortar mixture securing the cement block to other blocks. After at first trying to remove the stubborn block with a screwdriver, he decided it would be easier to pry it out with his fingers. To his delight, he saw that there was an open space, perhaps two feet deep, between the inner and outer walls. "They probably wanted to save money not filling it in," he said to himself.

After the initial excitement drained from his body, and with some reluctance, he placed the satchel in the open space. It was difficult parting with the jewels, not because millions of potential American dollars temporarily left his possession, but because of what the jewels had cost- fearful anticipation, a daring and risky robbery, and, worst of all, the death of his dear friend, Guido. "Oh, Guido," he said softly, "how I miss you."...

With the expertise of a craftsman, he returned the block to its original location and applied the adhesive around its edges, until he thought it was indistinguishable from any of the other blocks. He threw the small box, containing what he had used to remove and then seal the cement block, into the garbage container.

As Gaetano unlocked the stall door, a man barreled into him with such force that he was knocked against the rear wall. Before he could react, the stunned Gaetano felt the cold, sharp blade of a dagger pricking his chest. Thoughts about what happened to Guido raced through his mind, as he couldn't believe it was also happening to him. Then, he recognized the face of the man who this time was not wearing a red cap.

"Thought I forgot about you, Gaetano. That's your name, isn't it? I asked around about you. I've been following you since the last day on ship. Pretty good to find you among 2000 other people on the boat!"

"What...what do you want?" asked the stuttering Gaetano, knowing what he wanted, and so afraid that his legs were shaking.

"You know what I want. The diamonds and the other gems you stole from Vallone's. It's hard to think that you and that little donkey-eared freak could pull off such a heist. Must be dumb luck!"

Gaetano didn't know what to do with a dagger pushing against him and with this fierce-eyed, menacing killer demanding the jewels. He recalled the horrible vision of Guido being thrown into the ocean, and even though his body was shaking, his mind was yelling at him to resist and avenge the death of his childhood friend…he had to kill this man who killed Guido! This thought permeated every inch of his mind and body.

"I know you have the diamonds. Since your little geek friend didn't have them, you must have them. Now where are they? You don't want to end up like that ugly Sicilian, do you?"

Even though he was frozen with fear, Gaetano's mind told him that even if he told him where the jewels were, he would be killed, so there would be no witness.

"Where's that little bag you had when you came in here?"

As the killer looked around for the satchel, Gaetano tried to push the man's hand away from him. But the killer, too fast for him, swung his hand back and stabbed Gaetano in the chest. Gaetano stumbled, and as the man started to stab him again, Gaetano tried to speak: "Our father who art in…", and then darkness enveloped him…

There were many happy and sad stories that could be told about the 16 million immigrants entering the country from 1890 to 1930. One of the saddest was about the death of a basically good man, poor and desperate, but also kind and compassionate, who tried to survive a hard life and who almost reached the land of dreams…

Chapter 21
Revenge

Chen had enjoyed lunch with Kim and his wife hours earlier. It was a refreshing and nostalgic break from what he was going to do that night - kill Tan and "Q" and steal Tan's substantial crime proceeds which he knew was locked in his inner office safe.

To an ordinary person, killing at least two people in one night would be an extraordinarily horrendous act, but to Chen, the assassin, it was necessary to fulfill his vow to avenge his parents' death. Stealing all the money in Big Tan's safe, which Chen estimated would be hundreds of thousands of dollars, plus the possibility of obtaining and selling the stolen jewels, would make him a very, very rich man.

When he returned to Shanghai he would not only restore the life style he enjoyed when his parents were alive, but he would exceed it. In his mind danced visions of the ideal life: living in an expensive house, dining in exclusive restaurants, hobnobbing with the city's social elite and , foremost, enjoying sex with beautiful women of different nationalities - Chinese, Japanese, English, and an endless variety - all soon within his grasp. Maybe he might even try to become a respectable business man, eventually marry and have children, and forget his previous nightmarish existence as an assassin. With these thoughts, Chen was starting to resemble the Peter Chen who used to be.

Thus, in two days, he expected to complete his plans to be even richer- millions of dollars richer. Thanks to Kimmie's surveillance of Stanlee and eavesdropping on his conversations with Donna Martini, he learned what the private detective was going to do.

That Friday afternoon, Chen knew that Stanlee was going to search for the jewels that both men thought might be hidden somewhere in one of the buildings on Ellis Island. Chen, with pleasure, intended to kill Stanlee and take the jewels. Even if he didn't find the jewels, Stanlee would never leave the island alive.

Chen continued to daydream about resuming and improving on the well-to-do lifestyle of his youth. He kept envisioning living in a palatial modern home in the heart of Shanghai's wealthy district, driving a BMW or Mercedes Benz, like some of the rich dandies, and also socializing with some of the rich, beautiful upper-class women but not ruling out trysts with high-priced call girls or even the attractive bar girls in posh restaurants. But the sole emotion that dominated him now was revenge - a rage that had been bottled up for too many years and which was ready to explode.

That evening in Chinatown, near the famous narrow, north-south Mott Street, between Canal and Chatham Streets, a neighborhood that Chen favored because of its many Shanghai-like teahouses and restaurants, he parked his four-year old Cadillac in front of a nondescript building which belied the ornately furnished rooms on the second floor. He tapped out a seven-digit code on the keyboard, and the front door slowly opened. Chen, with his automatic and silencer in his pocket, walked quietly up the red-carpeted stairs.

Chen knew from what his father had told him that this second floor walk-up was only a fraction of Tan's vast holdings. Tan also owned property all over the world, veritable palaces in Grand Cayman Island, Hawaii, Hong Kong, Shanghai, and upper Westchester County in New York State.

But, for convenience, Tan preferred his relatively nearby Westchester Victorian-style mansion at the end of a long driveway and surrounded by isolating acres of trees. Chen knew about this mansion since in the first three months in Tan's employ, new recruits were required to chauffeur Tan daily from and to his Westchester home. That was when Chen was first personally exposed to Tan's brutal temper and anger. One driving maneuver that he disapproved of caused the arrogant Tan to spew a string of curses and belittling insults at Chen.

All of these memories of Tan's psychopathic behavior and the cruel merciless murder of his parents flooded Chen's mind as he moved catlike into the outer room. In this anteroom next to Big Tan's inner office, off limits to anyone unless specifically invited, were four of his Tong members and his regular chauffeur.

The four bodyguards, who were drinking heavily and playing Fantan, a Chinese card game, nodded at Chen. As if celebrating a special occasion exactly at midnight, they became more boisterous and grumbling and ordered the timid chauffeur to serve another round of drinks. The old short man quickly responded to each man's request.

"Q" nastily asked Li for a special drink they didn't have in order to taunt him. "Give me a Shanghai Sunset, Li. You know, with orange juice, Contreau, and bitters. And hurry up!" Laughing, as panic spread across the old man's face, he said, "I changed my mind. Forget it. Give me a Havana cigar and a glass of cold, not warm, sake." Li, knowing that the 6-5, 300 pound "Q" wasn't averse to sadistically pushing or hitting him when Tan wasn't around, quickly complied.

The others, not as mean or brutal as "Q," more politely chose one of the three numerous bottles of brand beer submerged with others in a huge wooden ice bucket: Heineken, Guinness, or Irish Kilkenny. The latter was a very popular beer not imported from Britain but from Shanghai at unnecessary expense by Tan, with other items, also from Shanghai. In the large outer office refrigerator there were also bottles or cans of Qingdaio, Shanghai's most famous domestic beer, the German beer Becks, Denmark's Carlsberg, and the Japanese beers, Suntory and Kirin. Tan liked to keep his subordinates happy and controllable by plying them with sufficient liquor, if requested, and low-level drugs.

After Li speedily brought them their drinks, they realized that Chen was still silently standing there-and to their astonishment, he was aiming his .45 automatic with silencer straight at them.

"Q" was first to respond. "What the hell are you doing, Chen, pointing that gun at us! Are you drunk?" Without hesitation, Chen in rapid succession shot each of the other three men in the upper chest. He felt some regret killing Tan's Japanese chauffeur because he knew what he, like him, must have gone through.

"Oh, my god! Are you crazy! What the hell have you done! Put down that goddamn gun!" "Q" started to get out of his chair which was barely large enough to hold his large body.

"Don't move, you fat pig."

"What's going on? Why are you insulting me! Why did you kill your own friends?"

"They're no friends of mine. And neither are you."

"What do you mean?" he said, now frightened. We've known each other for years. We're Tan's top assassins. We go back ten years!"

Speaking slowly and coldly, Chen said, "Do you remember killing Bien Chen, Tan's chief of laboratory operations, and his wife, ten years ago?"

"I've killed a lot of people, like you have, probably hundreds. How could I remember them…You said 'Chen.' Were they related to you? Is that it?"

"They were my father and mother," Chen said with such venom that a chill spread through "Q's" body. "You strangled them."

"Q" shook off the fear as best he could and said, "There are a lot of Chen's in China. Tan said to kill them, and I did. If I had known…"

"You still would have killed them. You didn't even know me then. You will kill your own father and mother, if Tan said so."

"Q" was on high alert, sweating and knowing that Chen was almost certainly about to kill him. "OK. OK. Relax. We can talk this out. You know what the job is. You get paid, like me, a lot of money for doing Tan's dirty work. You're just like me."

"Not quite like you. You enjoy killing your victims with a silk noose and then watching them gasp for air before they die. I've seen you do it many times-as you must have done to my parents."

"Q" moved slightly. "Sit down, 'Q,' or I'll blow a hole through your fat ugly stomach!"

"Look, Chen, I have a lot of money. It's yours. We can forget about this. Put down the gun, for god's sake!"

"Do you remember, "Q," when you hit my father on the head because he was protecting my mother and also trying to save his life?"

"Maybe, I don't remember. It was a long time ago."

"Well, I do. I see that bruise and that mark around their necks every day of my life."

"Really, Chen, I wouldn't have done it if I knew."

"As I just said, you didn't know me then. You know you're lying to save yourself. You knew Tan's wife, but you strangled her anyway."

"How did you know… for the…"

"I know."

At that moment, "Q" felt the panic and helplessness that his victims must have felt. Chen then shot him in the groin and relished - no, exulted - watching him suffer and scream in excruciating pain. Then he shot him again.

With tears streaming down his face, Chen murmured softly, "That's for you, Mom and Dad… that's for you… I kept my promise."

Chapter 22
Final Vow

"Q's" screams had alerted and alarmed Tan who opened the door of his inner office and was stunned to see so much blood and five dead bodies. Then he was even more surprised as he looked into the silencer of the gun held by Chen.

"What the hell… my god, what happened? Who did this? Did you do this? My god, why? Tell me!"

"No more orders, Tan. Now get back in your office, you disgusting little maggot!"

"Who do you think you're talking to, Chen. You work for me. You know who I am. I could have you killed for talking to me that way! And why did you kill my bodyguards?"

"And chauffeur," added Chen, who knew that Tan didn't mention his chauffeur because he regarded his Japanese employee with disdain and even inferior to his dim-witted Chinese bodyguards. "Without your bodyguards and your other hoodlums, you're nothing but a sniveling, pimple-faced old psychopath!"

"Why are you talking like that, Chen? Are you drunk? Are you on drugs? What the hell is the matter with you?"

There's nothing wrong with me Tan! And you know I don't do drugs like your doped-out customers and some of your thugs."

"Then why are you doing this? Are you insane?"

"Why, Tan, because ten years ago you destroyed my father, your chief chemist, because he wanted to retire and not work for you anymore. He retired despite your threats. You had your dead assassin - out there - strangle my father and mother. Don't deny it."

"You're the son of Bien Chen? I don't believe it. I knew he had a son but…"

"You never met me, and so it was easy to convince you to hire a young criminal from Hong Kong."

"You mean all these years you've been working for me, taking my money, and always planning, planning…"

"To kill you for having my parents murdered. Now it's your money I want-and maybe…maybe spare your miserable life."

"Can't we talk this over Peter? I'm a very rich man, as you know. I can give you whatever you want-make you a minor partner-or even a major one. But, don't shoot me!"

"Who said I was going to shoot you? All I want is all that money you have stashed in that safe there. Now open it!"

Tan, believing that he wasn't going to be shot, figured his life was more important than the money which could always be replaced. And later he would take care of Chen no matter where he tried to hide. Tan kneeled and with his fingers trembling moved the dial three times to the left and two times to the right until Chen heard the final click.

"Now, open the door, and for your sake, they'd better not be a gun in there. How much money is in there and don't lie to me-or else."

"About a million dollars. Two weeks plus of collections."

"I always knew you had something really going for you: drugs, prostitution, extortion. I heard you're now going into smuggling cigarettes. I understand that you think that you'll make more millions. Your father probably would be surprised that you improved on your inheritance. Without his starting all this, you'd probably be some bum in Shanghai or some coolie pulling a rickshaw in Hong Kong when they used to have them. That's what you're really suited for - pulling a little wagon with a passenger in it as they also used to do in Japan."

Tan silently pledged to kill Chen in the future for these insulting remarks. But his words and tone were conciliatory - actually pleading, for now. "Look, you take the money. You can go anywhere with it. I'll forget all about this as long as you don't shoot me."

"As I said, Tan, I'm not going to shoot you," Tan was still kneeling and facing the safe. Chen smiled, put away the automatic, and took a long silk cord from his pocket. "I just want you to know how it must have felt, Big Tan."

Chen circled the silk rope around his neck and tightened it as hard as he could. Tan, in panic, desperately tried to pull it off, but the effort was useless, and he soon slumped forward, hitting and severely bruising his head on the open door of the safe.

Chen, after killing six people, was as calm as he would be if he were sipping a cup of lucha', green tea, in a Shanghai teahouse or drinking Sakantas, a delicious mixture of strawberry liqueur, fresh strawberries, a sour mix, and sake-one of his favorites. For some strange and unexplainable reason, as he looked down at the hated Tan, he thought about the strawberry cocktail.

Chen stuffed the money, small and large bills, into four large canvas bags that Tan had used for transporting the money, with his bodyguards, to the bank. He would tomorrow mail three or four large boxes, topped and camouflaged with children's dolls, to Kimmie, care of his parents in Shanghai. He would tell Kimmie about expecting the boxes when he called him.

There should, however, be no difficulty with the Shanghai Customs, postal, or police authorities since thousands of letters, parcels and cargo containers each day passed easily through the two airports and East China Seaport. A great deal of imports was drugs, particularly opium and cocaine, and other similar contraband which passed without difficulty through Customs.

Chen, who had also worked briefly at the docks after his father retired, quickly learned that drug trafficking was a quasi-legal business. Some of the handlers, to augment their salaries, accepted bribes to overlook illegalities or to channel merchandise into the wrong hands; Tan was one of the major bribers. Unlike Shanghai, the rest of China tried to prevent, but not successfully, the illegal entry or use of drugs.

What finally caused Chen to quit his job on the docks was the exhausting, physically demanding nature of the job. Thanks to a college friend of Kimmie, he got a "white collar" job for a brief time as an Assistant Manager of a gambling house which offered not only gambling but also a host of prostitutes.

And now, thought Chen, as he carefully dragged the four canvas bags to his car, the next one to dispose of was that Private Detective.

Chapter 23
Entering the Past

In the late morning of that fateful Friday, Stanlee tried to imagine what it would have been like back in 1913, with immigrants crowding into barges, possibly from the same pier he had left, crossing the Hudson River, and landing almost an hour later at one of the many wharves at Ellis Island.

Gaetano Martini and the other immigrants must have first seen the Statue of Liberty on Bedloe's Island which was less than a mile to the south of Ellis Island. What a stirring, magnificent, and truly emotional sight it must have been to see the symbol of freedom and the promise of a better life! He could almost hear them, ninety-five years ago, yelling, crying, applauding first as they saw the Statue of Liberty from the deck of the steamship as it neared the port on the southern edge of Manhattan - and later when Ellis Island came into view a few minutes after the barges left the pier.

Stanlee suddenly felt a compassionate closeness to this strong, tall man, his girlfriend's ancestor, even though Gaetano had violated his own moral code and, out of poverty and desperation, was compelled to commit a major crime.

Stanlee's father, David, had helped in two ways. He had asked a still active New York City Police Sergeant to transport his son in a Police launch to Ellis Island. The Police Commissioner, a friend and a classmate of his father at the Police Academy thirty years ago, gave him a letter for his son which authorized his visit in case he was challenged by the two full-time guards patrolling the island which was closed to the public for the winter.

The police launch pulled close to the wharves. "I'll have to dock at the sturdiest spot, Steve. The wharves near the Reception area are either rotting or collapsing. What a shame. The wharves are in better condition further north since they're rebuilt and used for tourists only."

"It really is a shame," agreed Stanlee. So much neglect for such an historical place."

"Watch your step getting off."

"Thanks, Sergeant O'Connor. I appreciate it. I hope you don't get into any trouble using a Police launch to get me to the island."

"Don't worry about it. I'm in charge of the Police sea patrols in this area. The tourist boats won't be used until after the winter. They're in dry dock. Besides, anything for your father. He's a great guy. We've had many a brew together. He told me he and your mother are going next month on vacation to Alaska."

"I know. Thanks again, Sarge. As I said on the way here, please pick me up at this spot in about three hours. That'll be about four o'clock. I should be done by then. If not, please wait for me. See you then."

"OK. Don't worry about the time, Steve. I can wait a while. I see it's starting to snow. I hope that won't be a problem for you. It's not a problem for me. This baby (pointing to the open, half-decked motorboat,) can handle anything – snow, rain, rough waves. The worst that can happen is that you'll get a bit of snow on you."

"Fine, I'm just not used to snow on the first day in December." Stanlee was glad that Donna had suggested that he wear a sweater and heavy jacket since the weather prediction was for extreme cold and snow.

"Well, good luck whatever you're going to do. By the way, did you know the tourist guides say that this used to be called Gull Island by the Indians in the early 1600's? Hundreds of gulls used to swoop down on the oysters on the banks. That's one thing you don't have to worry about! Also, you're lucky. Since there won't be any tourists, the Ellis Island Museum is also closed for the winter. There'll be no tourists here, except you!"

He was astonished at the deplorable condition of the grounds. What used to be well-kept walks, lush green lawns, manicured bushes, and rows of flowers were now replaced by mounds of dirt, broken cement, paper litter, and strongly entrenched weeds. What still seemed to be impressive from a distance was the long, solid, spired Victorian-style Reception and Inspection Center. But, as he got closer to the building, he saw that the iron, brick, and cement facade was crumbling and deteriorating because of many decades of neglect. Near the entrance – if doors off its hinges and split into fragments can be called an entrance- was even more litter.

He knew generally what was inside the building after studying a copy of a layout. His father had convinced a clerk in the city Archives Department to photocopy the original architect's diagrams. What a retired Police Lieutenant's badge can do! The inside was in even poorer condition than the outside. The large entrance room, the cubicles upstairs, and the back rooms containing money exchange booths, a cafeteria, departure area, and utility rooms looked like a hurricane had swept through them and left all kinds of debris in its wake.

After he had walked through the entrance of the main building, something strange happened. In the semi-darkness, his mind seemed to be playing tricks on him as he imagined that he heard faint voices in a variety of native immigrant tongues. Were they from the year 1913? Were they voices of immigrants he heard- whispering, crying, fearing, despairing, questioning, threatening children to behave…Were these surreal shadows or apparitions swirling about him? He wondered what was happening to him!

Stanlee had never before experienced such ghost like hallucinations or perhaps they all somehow were an overwhelming emotional identification and compassion for the immigrants, particularly Gaetano! For a few seconds, he was motionless until the spectral sounds and shadows slowly receded from his over-active imagination, and he was back in the present. There was now only silence. No more ghosts of the past.

Rubbing his eyes as if to erase and confirm what really wasn't there, he took out the layout to locate the Washrooms. There was a lavatory (#1 and #2) on each side of the first floor entrance. On each side of the upper levels or balconies were Washrooms #3 to #6.

He knew that at the rear of the large room on the ground or main floor were high chairs and small desks used for interrogation by the Inspectors - the last hurdle for admission to the new land. Behind the main floor were the currency exchange, cafeteria, and washrooms #7 and #8.

Some of the immigrants who had been denied admission - for health or moral or criminal reasons - were devastated. They had left behind friends, relatives, jobs and, in addition, saw that their money so carefully saved was wasted. A few were so angry that they screamed, broke chairs, hurled foreign curses that fortunately most guards didn't understand, until they were finally subdued. All of those rejected were shipped back to their native country. It was terrible, they must have thought, to have come so far and then be turned away at the last moment.

He looked for Washroom #5, "Men," on his layout. The immigrants must have been grateful to have separate lavatories for men and women - unlike those aboard the immigrant ship - a fact revealed in other letters discovered in the trunk inherited by Donna's father.

If Stanlee's interpretation of the clues in Gaetano's letter was correct, the jewels should be hidden somewhere in Washroom #5 which was along the side and at the end of the upper east balcony. For the first time that he could remember, he had a brief but intensive panic attack-breathing hard and sweating.

As he walked cautiously up the unsound stairs to the balcony on the right, he tried to relax. He passed several rooms, which had been used for medical tests, and paused before the women's Washroom #6. Stanlee, with his nerves jumping, walked a few steps and then saw the large faded, black number 5 above the word "Men," at the top of the next door.

Chapter 24
The Search

Inside the number 5 lavatory cubicle, Stanlee took off his sweater and jacket and from the latter he removed a small toolbox. Looking excitedly around, before more thoroughly inspecting every inch of the small room, he tried to determine a likely place Gaetano would have hidden the jewels - if indeed he did so.

For almost a half hour, he examined the floor and walls for anything suggesting disturbance and a hiding place. The dust, paint chippings, and other bits of garbage, accumulated over decades, impeded his search.

Despairing, he thought it might all be a useless venture based on illusory information: Gaetano's letter and the mention of the jewels. What would be the odds of finding a fortune in jewels, probably now worth more than twenty-four million dollars, in a building in an island long forsaken by the government and the people? Fantasies were for motion pictures and not real life.

Perhaps the man who killed Guido (and later probably Gaetano) took the jewels? Or, could they have been thrown into the ocean by Gaetano to prevent Guido's murderer from getting them? All sorts of negative scenarios crossed Stanlee's mind.

As he was thinking, he happened to look down at a rectangular concrete block behind the commode and in the wall space below it. The edges of this particular block were brownish- gray unlike those of the other blocks which were surrounded by dirty white borders of cement. The blocks, coated originally with a bright white paint, were held together by cement except this one which apparently had a different putty or pasty substance around it. Muttering "It could be…it could be," he kneeled and then opened his newly purchased tool box which contained a small hammer, rubber gloves, screwdriver, and bricklayer's chisel.

With the hammer, he tapped gently around the block's putty-like edges and saw that it gave way more easily than aged cement would have. With the screwdriver, he tried to pry the block out, but eventually he found it faster and easier (like Gaetano) to use his fingers. The block came out and exposed an open space between the inner and outer walls.

Startled to actually see something there, he stared incredulously at a larger than usual strapless and zippered leather satchel bag with a handle. Snapping out of his mini-trance, he removed it gently and unzipped the heavy bag not knowing what to expect: twenty-four million dollars in jewels or bitter disappointment.

Brushing away the heavy covering of dust, he looked into the bag, placed there probably so hurriedly but carefully by Gaetano in 1913. A burst of colors came flying out at him: diamonds in many different hues-blue, green, purplish, red and green-and emeralds, red rubies, white pearls, green jade, and so many other gems and colors that they dazzled his senses. As if he were washing his hands, he ecstatically plunged them into the bag over and over again. Feeling them made him believe they really existed. It was incredible!

Then, he closed the satchel's zipper, put on his sweater and jacket, and in euphoria, with the satchel held tightly in his hand, he moved toward the front entrance and into the snow and coldness outside.

Chapter 25
Confrontation

In his excitement, he was hardly aware of trudging through the snow, now almost two inches deep, even though his feet were wet, and he was shivering. Suddenly, the elation vanished as if a sweet dream had turned into a nightmare. Chen, gun in his hand, came toward him from the side of the building.

"Well, Mr. Stanlee, we meet again. Thanks for doing my work for me. I assume that you found the jewels which must be in that bag you're holding so tightly."

Stanlee was speechless. Chen, with snow falling on him, looked like some ghostly white apparition holding death in his hand. In a moment, Stanlee's emotions had jumped from ecstasy to terror.

Chen, fortunately for the stunned Stanlee, was in a talkative, bragging mood. "I'm going to kill you, Stanlee, just like I killed the two park guards. Didn't you wonder where they were? Like I killed Tan, that scum who ordered the killing of my parents, and his assassin, that fat pig, "Q," who strangled my parents-two helpless, innocent people. After I kill you, my smart friend, I'll be going home and be a very rich man in Shanghai." Chen, by force of habit, slipped the silencer on his .45 automatic, which was unnecessary since there was no one on the island to hear gunshots.

"Wait a minute, Chen," said the panicking Stanlee, stalling for time. "Why did you save my life in Tan's office only to kill me now?"

"A good question. I'll consider it the last wish of a man about to die. Don't say I never did anything for you," he said sarcastically.

Chen, in talking to Stanlee, for some reason was caught momentarily in the past as he remembered a painful and unerasable time in his life. He told Stanlee how Tan had ruined his father's life. "Tan needed my father, his chief lab specialist, who was an expert in analyzing and sometimes refining imported drugs." Stanlee even in his alarmed state couldn't help admiring Chen's clear and organized choice of words and his obvious expert familiarity with the English language.

"My father, in his seventies, wanted to retire and did so, unfortunately at a very modest monthly stipend." Chen then said that the vengeful Tan threatened creditors to collect as many debts as they could from his father. "We were forced to move from an expensive house in a good neighborhood to a cheap shack of a place in the poorest part of Shanghai. I'm sure you wouldn't know about things like that." He paused and looked intently at Stanlee as if looking for signs of compassion. There were none.

"A few months later, we met Mr. Chang in a supermarket. My father began to chat with him, and they found that they enjoyed each other's company. Mr. Chang used to be a Police Lieutenant, in Shanghai, a police officer like your father. After he retired, to keep active, he became a Private Detective, like you."

Chen looked into Stanlee's blue eyes, and wondered if circumstances were different would he and Stanlee have been friends. Something about Stanlee reminded him of himself the way he was years ago, in a different time, a different place.

"Am I boring you, Stanlee?"

"No, no. It's very interesting." (which was the truth). Stanlee, trying not to panic, also was trying to think of a way to get out of this alive, but his situation looked hopeless.

"Mr. Chang, when he knew our money was almost gone near the end of the month, used to bring us bags of groceries and sometimes a bottle or two of wine, usually Chardonnay, which my father liked, and Japanese Sake, a rice wine which we liked served hot. He was a very kind man, like my father. In fact, he was like a second father to me." Chen (and also Stanlee) couldn't figure out why he was talking so much. Was it venting, confession, or justification?

"Too much detail for you, Stanlee?" He didn't wait for an answer since he realized he was talking about his past life which probably was beyond Stanlee's interest and understanding.

"What's all this got to do with me, Chen?" Stanlee felt sweat, even in the extreme coldness, running down the nape of his neck.

"Somehow, lucky for you, you reminded me of Mr. Chang, who also was a private detective like you, who helped us when we really needed it. It was strange, but I felt sparing your life was a way of repaying a debt that I owed Mr. Chang.

That's when I made up the story about us both looking for the jewels." The look of menace again appeared in his eyes and face.

"Now that I answered your question, perhaps in more detail than you thought or as I wished, it's your turn. In a way, I feel sorry about this."

For the second time that month, he aimed the automatic at Stanlee's head…

Chapter 26
Fatal Error

"Give me the bag, Stanlee."

Stanlee later realized that this was when Chen made his fatal mistake. Instead of telling him to drop the bag and move back a few feet before killing him, Chen reached greedily and impatiently for the satchel which Stanlee raised toward him.

As Chen briefly shifted his gaze to the bag, Stanlee swung it as hard as he could at the gun and then at Chen's head. The unexpected blow knocked the automatic and then Chen into the snow. Chen, rubbing his forehead and slightly dazed, groped vainly for the gun in the snow, and when he couldn't find it, took out a long dagger from a sheath inside his jacket.

As he was getting up, Chen slashed forcefully through Stanlee's jacket and sweater and cut him across his stomach before Stanlee kicked him so viciously in the groin that Chen screamed in pain and dropped the dagger. Before it disappeared into the snow, Stanlee retrieved it. With a fury that he never knew he possessed, he plunged the dagger over and over again into Chen's chest. When he didn't move, Stanlee stopped and tried to remove the dagger, but it was too deeply imbedded in Chen's chest. He looked at the lifeless body and then his face, once menacing and cruel, but now strangely peaceful and youthful looking.

Stanlee thought that Chen, from what he just heard, probably was a good man in his youth until the ugliness of revenge drove him to "the dark side," as Stanlee's father used to say. Revenge, propelled by grief and rage, can create monsters. His father also had once told him after years of dealing with criminals and the good guys that "There's a thin line between good and evil."

Exhausted, cold, and dizzy, and with blood dripping rapidly from his stomach down his legs, Stanlee, through the haze of delirium, looked at the spots of blood surrounding Chen's body in the snow and thought he saw diamonds that resembled strawberries-and then he lost consciousness.

Epilogue

Sergeant O'Connor had found Stanlee lying unconscious in the snow. He picked up the satchel and then carried him to the Police launch. As he raced in the now heavily falling snow to the Manhattan Police docking wharf, he called for an ambulance to transport the near-death Stanlee to N.Y Downtown Hospital where, the attending doctor said, the transfusion of four units of blood saved his life. As Stanlee was being ministered to, the doctor said he kept mumbling "They're strawberries and diamonds, they're strawberries and diamonds…"

With the parents half asleep and worrying that Steve was still in a coma, Donna sat in a chair with her head on his bed, alternately sobbing and praying until she fell asleep. Early that morning, she woke up when she felt his hand on her head. "I love you, Donna," he said. Ecstatic and relieved that he was conscious, she said, "I love you too," and kissed him fervently but gently.

"Donna, I had the strangest dream. Oh, don't cry. I'm OK. Don't cry. Please don't cry… You remember what you told me when we first met? You said your story was strange and unbelievable. Well, so is this. I dreamt that Gaetano was standing by my bed, next to a little fellow, and he said, in English, 'We're happy for both of you.'" She started to cry again, and then so did he.

Donna and Steve were later married, and they had three children: David, Timothy, and Donna Jean. Sergeant O'Connor was the godfather to their first child, David.

With Donna's approval, Steve had (without guilt) retained forty of the largest and most expensive stolen diamonds as his fee and for almost losing his life. After all, Donna had said. "We could have kept them all!"

Steve also sold his personal collection of diamonds and with the sizable reward given to him by the surprised but grateful and still existing Vallone Brothers Corporation, they bought a great deal of property, including a large house near the Sound on the North Shore of Long Island and one in the Grand Cayman Islands.

On their honeymoon, they went to Alaska. Stanlee retired from the private detective business and is now a college instructor and novelist.

The CEO, the great-great grandson of the founder of the Vallone Brothers Corporation, suspected for a long time, without proof, that not all of the jewels were recovered. Since the company inventories for 1913 were either lost or misplaced, his suspicions could never be confirmed.

♦♦♦

It should be noted that Donna and Steve Stanlee, for the rest of their lives, would never forget the story of the two immigrants, Gaetano and Guido, who almost…almost made it to the land of dreams…the Unites States of America.

Postscript

I can tell you now that years ago when I was in Prizzi, Sicily, on leave from my U.S Army post in La Rochelle, France, I met some of the descendants, including friends as well as relatives, of Gaetano and Guido.

Fortunately, a former cab driver in New York City who returned to Prizzi, his birthplace, initially told me the story of Gaetano and Guido.

At first, his tale seemed embellished and melodramatic-and I must admit, unrealistic-but after a while the heroic drama of their sad and desperate lives so overwhelmed me that I had to write the almost unbelievable story of my distant ancestor, Gaetano, and his dear friend, Guido.

Did the citizens of Prizzi exaggerate their story in order to please, impress, or entertain their American friend?

You can decide for yourself, and look it up-as I did.

S.S.

♦♦♦

www.ingramcontent.com/pod-product-compliance
Lightning Source LLC
Chambersburg PA
CBHW060528310726
48982CB00002B/466

* 9 7 8 1 4 2 6 9 0 0 2 3 5 *